heart side

Published by SMPUBLISHINGCO
First edition, 2026

heart
side
a novel
Samantha M. Miller

The Heartside Playlist

These are the songs I listened to while writing Heartside. They inspired the mood, the feelings, and a lot of the moments in this story.

If you'd like, you can listen along as you read by scanning the QR code below.

For the hearts that have been patient,
and the ones still learning to receive
may this story remind you that healing is not the end of love,
but the doorway that leads you to it.

One
Amelia

The alarm clock went off on my nightstand, and I shot up, feeling as if I'd just been run over by a truck.

It took a moment for the realization to fully settle in that this was yet another morning in the James household. They always started the same way as I stared at the rays of sunshine that streamed through thin curtains, casting a gentle glow over my bedroom. I reached out to silence the alarm on my phone, groaning slightly. It was only six o'clock, and another busy day already lay ahead of me.

Still, the day started right.

I glanced over at Sophie, my six-year-old daughter, still peacefully asleep in her small bed across the room. The one-bedroom apartment that we shared was less than what I wanted to give to her, but in moments like these, I didn't mind the closeness that it allowed. After all, she'd only stay so small for so long. In only a decade or so, she'd be stepping out into the world to live her own life, and I'd be watching her from afar. The thought alone was so depressing.

For now, I allowed myself to enjoy the sight of my entire world, curled up in the small bed, amongst all the pillows and her floral duvet. Her soft chestnut curls framed her small face, and her big blue eyes, usually so full of curiosity, were closed, hidden beneath her long lashes. One hand held the teddy bear I'd won for her at the fair a year ago, her favorite ever since. The dimples that always showed when she smiled were now quietly tucked away in her cheeks, and I couldn't wait for her to wake up and for them to be on full display. It was impossible not to smile at the sight as I watched her chest rise and fall with the steady rhythm of childhood dreams. I envied her ability to sleep so soundly.

I couldn't remember the last time I'd gotten a proper sleep like that.

I let myself linger in the moment for a second longer, then I quietly slipped out of bed and tiptoed to the bathroom to start my day. As soon as the hot water touched my skin, my muscles loosened, and I began feeling more awake. In my head, I went over everything I had to do today, drop Sophie off at school, head to work, grab groceries on the way back, then pick up my little girl again. That was when my favorite part of the day would start, when I got to listen to her tell me all about her day while we shared a meal together.

It wasn't long before I managed to pry myself away from the warm comfort of my shower, stepping out to get dressed. My work attire was the same for the most part, a tailored blouse and slacks. The only thing I'd usually play around with was the color combinations, but even with that, I'd stick to the safe options.

I glanced at my reflection, noting my early-thirties appearance. Sophie was, undoubtedly, the reason behind the few smile lines that I had across my face. The past six years, no matter how difficult at times, had been filled with so much laughter that it was guaranteed to leave a mark on my face. The same chestnut brown hair with natural highlights that my daughter had fell into loose waves around my face, and my hazel eyes, unsurprisingly, looked tired. That was nothing a little bit of concealer couldn't hide, though.

After all, as a marketing manager at Elite Source, a prominent firm in Houston, I needed to look professional and put together, even when I often felt anything but. By the time I brought my routine to an end and emerged back into the bedroom, Sophie was stirring. Her eyes fluttered open, and she gave me a sleepy smile.

"Morning, Mommy," she mumbled.

"Good morning, sweetheart," I replied, bending down to kiss her forehead. The warmth of her skin momentarily lingered against my lips, and then it remained there, even when I pulled back. "Ready to get up and have some breakfast?" She nodded, rubbing her eyes. "You get out of the bed and get ready, and I'll get started on your food, all right?"

Sophie nodded and hopped out of bed, ready for her usual morning routine, with her clothes prepared last night. I, on the other hand, headed to the kitchen to prepare our usual morning meal, cereal for Sophie and a strong cup of coffee for me. My eyes wandered slowly around the familiar space, taking in every detail that had become part of our lives. When we first moved in, the walls were empty, plain, and colorless, and the counters looked cold, almost as if no one could really live here. It felt more like a temporary stop than a home. Now, the walls were filled with photographs of Sophie and me, and the fridge was covered entirely in her endless drawings. I made sure to buy fresh flowers every week; it was a small ritual, but it breathed life into the apartment. The mismatched tiles on the kitchen floor, once something I found distracting, had become a pattern I knew by heart. Scattered all around were Sophie's little knick-knacks she always left behind, a doll shoe under the couch, a bead bracelet on the coffee table, and a crayon on the floor by the door.

Then Sophie came into view, already dressed and with her teeth brushed, her smile stretching from ear to ear. I couldn't help but smile back, raising an eyebrow playfully as I set her bowl down on the counter.

"Do you want some strawberries with your cereal today?" I asked pulling a container of fresh berries from the fridge.

"Yes, please," she said, sliding into her chair. As I sliced the strawberries, my mind drifted for a moment, pulling me back into old memories. I thought about the life we had then and the life we had now. The difference between the two felt like night and day. Moments like these, no matter how small, added structure and predictability, something I desperately needed in my life.

"Good luck with your science project today, sweetheart. I can't wait to hear all about it when you get home," I told her as I set down her breakfast and took a long sip of my coffee. Watching her grow, step by step, had been the greatest gift. Every milestone, big or small, felt like a celebration, and moments like this, when she was nervous, reminded me how important it was for to be her constant cheerleader. A girl like her could do anything in this world, and it was my job to make sure she always knew that.

"Thanks, Mommy," she murmured, her nose scrunching just a little. The project wasn't anything huge—just showing the solar system, but to her, it was everything, which meant, of course, that it was everything to me too.

"Do you really think it will go well?" she asked, and I caught the tiny thread of doubt in her voice. Still, I couldn't stop the smile that spread across my face.

"Of course, Soph. You've done an amazing job. I couldn't be prouder of you."

Her small shoulders eased as the tension melted away, and she dove into her breakfast. Between bites, she chattered about everything and nothing all at once, and I found myself lost in the sound until it was time for us to leave.

"Now let's get your backpack. We don't want to be late," I prompted her, and she nodded, dashing into the bedroom to grab it before it was time for us to leave. The chatter between us continued all the way to her school, where I dropped her off with a kiss.

Then I headed to Elite Source. This was my time to recharge before I dug into my daily tasks, and there were a lot of them. My job as a marketing manager was demanding, but I took pride in my work. It was a career I had built through years of hard work and dedication, balancing the demands of the job with the responsibilities of being a single mother.

As always, I got caught in the morning traffic, waiting a good fifteen minutes before the line of cars began to move. Still, I felt calm, with the soft hum of the radio filling the car, as warm sunlight slipped through the glass, brushing against my skin.

Once the traffic cleared, it took me only another twenty minutes to reach the office building downtown. Its sleek glass façade rose high above me, seven stories tall, and the sunlight bounced off its surface in a sharp reflection. I pulled into the garage, and then the click of my shoes against the cement echoed as I crossed the wide space and stepped into the waiting elevator.

The ride upward was smooth, climbing four floors before the doors slid open. I stepped out and was greeted by the familiar view I had seen countless times before. The grey walls were decorated with motivational posters and framed success stories from past campaigns. These were all subtle reminders of the work we had done and the difference our team had made, and I was proud to be a part of it. A few green plants stood in corners and along the edges of the space, softening the room's otherwise polished look. The dark furniture, with its straight, clean lines, gave the office a professional tone, though the touches of green kept it from feeling too cold.

At the far end stood the door to my office, and in front of it was the neat desk where my assistant sat. She noticed me at once, rising to her feet. She gave me a small smile, her red-painted lips curving just slightly. Today she wore a white blouse tucked into a fitted black pencil skirt, and it suited her perfectly.

"Good morning, Amelia," Lisa said, handing me my cup of coffee. She already knew how I liked it and when to have it ready for me. "You have a meeting with the team at nine to discuss the new marketing campaign for Poise."

"Thanks, Lisa," I replied, setting my bag down and powering up my computer. I had a few emails to catch up on before the meeting, including one from my boss, Mr. Thompson, outlining the goals for our latest project. Poise, a company focused on women's wellness products, was quickly becoming a real success in the market, and they were eager for their marketing to match that growth. Over the past few months, their rapid rise had made them one of our most promising and important clients, which meant my schedule was more crowded than ever. I was constantly juggling calls, emails, and project updates, making sure every detail met their high expectations.

Still, that didn't mean I didn't enjoy the work. Even on the toughest days, there was satisfaction in knowing that every effort I put in mattered. My hours were filled with back-to-back meetings, strategy sessions, and creative brainstorming, all designed to push campaigns forward and deliver exceptional results. Despite the stress, I thrived on the challenge. It was in these moments of intense focus and collaboration that I felt most alive, most like the person I used to be before life became so complicated.

By lunchtime, I needed a break. I headed downstairs to the cafeteria and picked up my usual, a salad and a tall iced coffee. It was my go-to lunch, something light but enough to carry me through the rest of the day until I could have dinner with Sophie. I glanced at my phone, checking the time. Around now, she would be standing in front of her classmates, presenting her solar system project. It was heavily simplified, of course, but it still made me proud, nonetheless. I crossed my fingers for her, wishing I could be there to see it, but I knew I'd be hearing all about it later today.

I settled into a quiet corner of the break room, opening the book I had brought along. It was a small attempt to distract myself from the constant thoughts running through my head. Normally, losing myself in a few chapters worked well enough, but today even the familiar escape of words couldn't entirely pull my mind away.

A familiar knot lingered low in my stomach. Usually, when everything seemed to be going smoothly, something unexpected would snap through it and turn everything upside down. Even amid routine and small joys, that shadow of fear refused to leave.

After lunch, it was back to the grind. The afternoon was filled with client calls and project updates, but at least it passed more quickly. Before I knew it, it was time to pick up Sophie from school. I wrapped up my work, grabbed my bag, and headed out, thankful that the traffic was usually be better on my way back home. I made a quick stop at the grocery store on my way to her school, grabbing a few things we'd need for dinner. Then, with my bags tucked in the car, I could hardly contain my excitement as I pulled up in front of her school. It was a familiar part of my routine, one I had done countless times before, but no matter how many pickups there were, that little rush of joy never faded. Seeing her waiting for me, her face lighting up as she spotted our car, was the best part of my day.

"Mommy!" she exclaimed, running to me with open arms.

I crouched to give her a big hug, spinning her in my arms. "Hi, sweetheart! How was school today?"

"It was great! And my project went just fine," she said, nodding proudly. "I only made one tiny, teeny mistake when I was showing it to my friends." Even so, her eyes sparkled with excitement, and it warmed my heart to see her so happy.

"That's okay, sweetheart. Mistakes are how we learn," I said as I helped her into the car. She scrunched up her little face and looked at me with suspicion.

"Does that mean you also make mistakes at work, Mommy?"

I couldn't help but chuckle before I could even think it through. "All the time, baby," I admitted, sliding into the driver's seat and starting the car.

The plan had been tacos for dinner, but Sophie insisted on pizza. It was nearly impossible to say no to her, so pizza it was. After we ate, the evening flowed in its usual rhythm—homework, a little playtime, all while laughter filled the living room. It was a routine I cherished and that never seemed to change, and I wasn't ready to let it go anytime soon.

By the time she was in bed, all tucked in, a sleepy smile crossed her face, but that didn't stop her gaze from hopefully lifting to meet mine.

"Mommy, can we read the princess story again?"

"Of course," I said, reaching for the book. It was her favorite story, about a princess searching for love and finding it in the most unexpected of boys. I had read it to her dozens of times, yet she always asked for it again and again.

Almost without fail, she never made it through the entire story. By the time we reached the middle, she would be curled up against my shoulder, already fast asleep. I smiled softly, placing a gentle kiss on her forehead, and slipped out of her room, leaving her to dream peacefully.

I settled onto the couch with a cup of tea, and I allowed myself a moment of quiet reflection. Life was busy and often exhausting, but I felt a sense of purpose. It had taken me a while to find it, given how difficult life had been for years now.

Ever since Brad, Sophie's dad, walked out on me when I was pregnant, leaving me to raise her on my own, I hadn't felt I could open up and take on another relationship. Raising Sophie alone left little room for romance, and sometimes I wondered where love fit into my life now, if it would ever find a spot in this chaos at all. The thought snuck some heaviness into my heart, but I did my best to chase it away.

To soothe my mind, I turned on the TV and settled in to watch my favorite comfort movie, Pride and Prejudice. The familiar scenes unfolded, and I let the timeless story carry me away. Eventually, I drifted off to sleep on the couch, the words of Mr. Darcy's proposal lingered in my dreams, and I could only hope that a love like that was waiting for me somewhere along the way.

Two
Amelia

The next morning, after dropping Sophie off at school, my routine brought me back to Elite Source. The morning buzz was already in full swing when I arrived there. Lisa greeted me at the door with a fresh cup of coffee, like she always did, and instantly started giving me the rundown for the day. I thanked her and greeted my colleagues as I made my way to my office, ready to tackle the tasks ahead. While I was catching up on emails, my phone buzzed with a message notification. I glanced at the screen and saw it was from our group chat, "The Three Musketeers," which consisted of me and my two best friends, Victoria and Anastasia.

My mood instantly perked up. If there was anyone in this world who had this effect on me, aside from Sophie, it was those two.

Victoria:

Good morning, besties! Amelia, we have some news to share. Anastasia and I have been thinking and were planning something fun for my birthday. How do you both feel about a girls' weekend in Vegas in the third week of May?

Anastasia:

We know it's short notice, but Victoria scored us a great deal on a vacation package, and it's too good to pass up! We can use a little girls' getaway :)

I stared at the message, a mixture of excitement and hesitation swirling in my chest. A weekend getaway in Vegas sounded amazing, but the logistics of leaving Sophie and stepping away from work were daunting. I had a month to find a sitter for Sophie, but it was Victoria's birthday, and I could not let her down.

Me:

Wow, you guys! Vegas?! Vic, it's your birthday., of course, I have to be there to celebrate with my best girls. But first, let me arrange everything with my parents and check if they can watch Sophie for me. I'll let you know!

Victoria:

I'll let you know? Amelia, that is code for I'm politely rejecting the offer . Oh! Also, I wanted to share that I got us a connection in Vegas, a promoter guy named Jake. One of my former college roommates, who hooked up with him, works out there, and he says he can get us into the hottest pool parties and clubs. If we're interested, of course.

Anastasia:

Yeah, Amelia! Victoria has this birthday trip planned! You have no choice but to join us! We need you there, Three Musketeers, remember?

I bit my lip, thinking it over. A getaway with Victoria and Anastasia would be so much fun. Besides, they were right. we could all use a break. Maybe this was exactly what I needed to recharge, even if it was nothing like my idea of a vacation. Most of the time, my world revolved around Sophie and what she wanted to do, and I never minded it for a second. Her happiness was my happiness, always. But just this once, it felt like it might be nice to do something purely for myself, something entirely my own.

Me:

> You're right. Okay, okay. It does sound like fun. I'll figure something out. Fuck it, let's do it. Count me in!

I hit send before I could overthink it, a smile spreading across my face. Sometimes, you just had to leap before giving yourself any time to change your mind, and if anyone deserved that leap of faith like this from me, it was my best friends.

Victoria, Anastasia, and I had known each other since we were kids, living in the same River Oaks subdivision in Houston. We dubbed ourselves the Three Musketeers and have been in each other's lives ever since. Our bond was cemented one day on the playground when we were nine. I was being bullied by Big Shelly, who earned her nickname because she was nearly twice the size of an average nine-year-old. Shelly had cornered me near the swings, taunting me and pushing me around.

Just when I thought I would have to face her alone, Victoria and Anastasia, who were also on the playground, saw what was happening. Without a moment's hesitation, they jumped in to help, standing up to Shelly and fighting her off. From that day forward, we swore to always have each other's backs, and that was a promise we stuck by through good and hard times.

Victoria was the life of every party, effortlessly drawing people in. Her long, flowing blonde hair cascaded down her back in loose waves, and her bright blue eyes shimmered with energy and excitement wherever she appeared. She had a knack for fashion, often wearing bold and colorful outfits that matched her vibrant personality. Over the years, her wild streak had tempered slightly, but she remained the same fun-loving and fiercely loyal friend I had always known. As an event planner, her job perfectly suited her talent for organizing and creating memorable experiences.

Anastasia, on the other hand, was the calm, steady presence in our trio. With raven-black hair that fell in silky waves to her shoulders and deep, soulful brown eyes, she exuded inner strength and resilience. Petite and graceful, she still belied a fierce determination. She favored elegant, and understated styles, choosing classic pieces that reflected her timeless beauty. As a nurse, her compassionate nature made her perfect fit for the job. She had a way of grounding me when I felt overwhelmed, always ready with a listening ear and sound advice.

Life hadn't been easy for me over the past couple of years. When Brad left and never looked back, I was broken into a million pieces, to the point where I wasn't sure if I would ever be able to pick myself back up again. It was a painful chapter in my life, one that left deep scars, In his absence, Victoria and Anastasia had stepped up, filling the void with their support and love.

They were the glue holding the pieces of my shattered world together. When Sophie was first born, and I thought I would never sleep again, they took turns helping me watch over her so I could close my eyes for a while. When I was sick and in need of a warm meal, they showed up with food without me ever having to ask. And when everything became too much, they'd take Sophie for a little while, giving me the chance to breathe. That was the kind of friends they were; ones I could always count on. Doing this for them felt like the least I could do. We all deserved it, a little time together, just for us.

Besides, with both Victoria and Anastasia technically single gals and having no children of their own, Sophie had grown accustomed to being spoiled by her two loving aunts. They showered her with attention, filling her life with joy and laughter. Whether it was baking cookies together, going to the movies, or just hanging out at home, Victoria and Anastasia made sure Sophie knew she was deeply loved, and that was one thing I could never forget.

Anastasia:

No going back on your word, you know?
This is a done deal now.

Victoria:

Yeah! And we do mean that. You've bailed
on us a few times in the past, but you
need a break. Away from everything and
everyone. You know we love Sophie and
would die for her, but you need to be
yourself again, and not just her lovely mom.
If even for a weekend, girl.

I pondered her words for a long moment. When was the last time I felt like myself? Motherhood had undoubtedly been such a beautiful part of my life, but there were versions of me long forgotten, ones I sometimes recall in small moments here and there. Perhaps this weekend that they planned could be one of those occasions. A small smile crossed my face again.

Me:

Deal. No going back.

The rest of the day flew by in a whirlwind of meetings and project updates. As I left the office and headed to pick up Sophie, I could clearly feel the excitement that had taken root in my chest. A weekend in Vegas with Vic and Stas would be a much-needed break from routine and motherhood, I realized, and an opportunity for me to finally feel like myself again. Since the two of them had been the ones to come up with this idea, I had no doubt they already had a plan in mind. I could practically predict it: margaritas and dresses I would never usually choose for myself, but that they'd insist looked perfect on me. Normally, I would have put up a little resistance, brushing it off with excuses or protests, but this time was different. I found myself actually looking forward to it all, maybe a little too much to even think about saying no.

At dinner, Sophie talked about her day while I made a mental checklist of everything I needed to prepare for the trip. I hadn't told her about the trip yet, and as I listened to her chatter about her day, I found it almost impossible to bring myself to say the words. The guilt hit me hard. I couldn't even remember the last time the two of us had been apart for more than a single day.

"Are you okay, Mommy?" Sophie asked, her big eyes studying me, and the guilt only dug deeper. I forced a smile, even though it felt weighed down. In my mind, I knew this trip was a good thing, something I shouldn't feel bad about.

But my heart wouldn't accept that. It reminded me, over and over, that it was just the two of us, no one else.

"Yes, baby. Of course. Just had a long day and a few things I need to figure out," I said softly, reaching over to ruffle her hair. She nodded and gave me one of her easy smiles. Simple as that and we carried on with our usual evening routine until I finally tucked her into bed.

When the house fell quiet afterward, I sank into the couch, but the guilt clung to me tighter than before, wrapping around me until it was all I could think about. Eventually, I realized there was nothing left to do but pick up my phone and dial Anastasia's number.

"Hey, Stas," I said when she answered. I didn't even give her a chance to speak before I spilled what was on my mind. "So why am I feeling nervous about this trip and leaving Sophie with my parents? And asking to take time off from work?" I exhaled softly, pinching the bridge of my nose between my fingers. "I know this is what people *should* do and there's nothing wrong with it, but I still can't help myself."

"Everything that you feel is completely normal, especially for single moms," Anastasia replied, her voice filled with warmth and understanding. "You deserve time for yourself, too. You know your mom loves spending time with Sophie. She loves her Nana too, and it's been a while since the last time the two of them spent some time together. But you've been so stressed with everything going on, and you've barely had any time for yourself, let alone your best friends. It's time we change that."

I smiled weakly, grateful for her attempt to cheer me up.

"I know, but I can't help feeling like I'm abandoning her." I said. The words hung in the air between us, itching at me.

I swallowed the lump that formed in the back of my throat, trying my best to force more words past my lips. "That will pass, won't it?"

Anastasia sighed softly. "Amelia, you are the best mom to Sophie. She knows how much you love her, and a weekend away won't change that. It's healthy for you to take a break and recharge. You deserve it, girl. Let's be honest, you've been working so hard and have barely had the time to breathe. You need this trip." She paused for a long moment. "It will pass the moment you grab that first margarita."

"I guess you're right," I admitted, feeling some of the tension release from my shoulders. "I just worry."

"It's normal to worry, but trust me, Sophie will have a blast with your mom, and you'll come back feeling refreshed and ready to take on the world again."

I lingered for a long moment, letting the words sink into my mind, until I held onto them so tightly that no guilt could take them away. I took a long sip of my tea, leaning back against the couch as I exhaled softly.

"You always know how to make me feel better, Stas."

With Sophie's schoolwork and my job demanding so much of my attention, I often forgot what it felt like to let loose and have fun. This trip was a chance to reconnect with my friends and, perhaps with a part of myself I had lost along the way.

***

The weeks leading up to the trip were a chaos and anticipation. Victoria kept us updated with her meticulous planning, sharing details about the flights, hotel accommodations, and the exciting itinerary she had put together. Meanwhile,

Anastasia checked in with us regularly, making sure we were all set and offering reassurance whenever my nerves got the best of me.

I had been given just one task: to relax, not let the guilt take over, and to pick outfits that pushed me a little outside my usual comfort zone. So far, I was managing all of it surprisingly well. I could feel myself unwinding bit by bit, even catching myself looking forward to what was ahead.

Sophie, of course, couldn't have been more supportive from the moment I finally told her. All it took was the promise of a teddy bear from Vegas, and her face lit up like it was the best news she'd ever heard. On top of that, she was thrilled about spending time with her grandparents—something that didn't happen as often as either of us would have liked. Her excitement made everything feel easier, and for the first time in a long time, I allowed myself to believe that maybe this trip really was the best thing I could do for myself.

My parents eagerly agreed to take care of Sophie for the weekend, reassuring me that they were looking forward to spending quality time with their granddaughter as well. It eased my mind knowing Sophie would be in good hands, but still, that pang of guilt returned as I kissed her goodbye Thursday morning, standing right in front of the airport. She, on the other hand, was smiling from ear to ear as she stared up at me.

"Why do you look sad, Mommy? You should be excited! You get to fly in a plane and spend the weekend with Auntie Victoria and Anastasia," she said with a nod. I stared at her for a long moment, wondering when she had grown up so much. For a moment, it felt like time was slipping between my fingers, and there was nothing I could do about it.

"I'm just going to miss you, sweetie, that's all," I admitted, offering another smile. I hoped this one would be more convincing than the last. She wrapped her tiny arms around me, holding me for a long moment. "You be good for Nana and Papa, okay?"

Sophie nodded. "Of course, Mommy. Have fun on your trip."

"Thank you, sweetheart. I love you," I said, holding her close for a moment. It was so hard to let her go, but somehow, I managed to pry myself away from her arms. My chest ached as I pulled back, When I finally lifted my gaze, it landed on my mom. Almost as if she could feel every worry running through me, her expression softened in that way only she could manage. People had always told me I would look just like her one day, Standing there, I hoped they were right. The gentle lines on her face and the kindness and warmth in her eyes were so calming to see. If that was my future, there was nothing I could want more.

"Don't worry, Amelia. We'll have a wonderful time, won't we, Sophie?" my mom said, smiling down at her.

"Yeah!" Sophie cheered, waving at me. I gave her one more quick kiss, then I grabbed my suitcase and headed out toward the entrance. I looked back at Sophie one more time, unable to help the smile that curved my lips as I spotted her holding my mom's hand, smiling widely, like she didn't have a single worry on her mind.

Finally, I stepped inside and made my way toward the check-in desks. My eyes wandered through the busy space, searching the crowd for familiar faces. All around me, people hurried past with suitcases rolling behind them, each one eager to get to their own destination. Overhead, announcements echoed through the airport, blending with the hum of voices of footsteps.

I kept looking, my heart beating a little faster, until at last my gaze finally landed on my best friends waiting on the other side. The moment I spotted them, I hurried forward, their faces lighting up instantly.

"Amelia!" Victoria squealed, hurrying forward to wrap me in a tight hug. Her long blonde hair was pulled back into a high ponytail that swayed with her movements, and her bright blue eyes stayed locked on mine, sparkling with excitement. She wore a bold hot pink outfit that immediately caught the eye, standing out in the sea of travellers bustling around us, but of course, that was Victoria. It suited her perfectly. "Are you ready for this?"

Beside her, Anastasia offered me a warm smile. Her dark hair framed her face in soft waves, falling gracefully over her shoulders, and her deep brown eyes studied me with quiet care, as though searching for even the slightest trace of hesitation. But there wasn't any. Not this time. "A little girls' getaway is just what we all need, don't you think?"

"You're damn right." I returned their hugs, feeling excitement finally pump through me at last. "I can't wait. This will be good for all of us. I can feel it."

Three

Amelia

We stepped off the plane and into the warm, vibrant air of Las Vegas, immediately greeted by the hustle and bustle of McCarran International Airport. The energy was infectious, and a constant hum of excitement seemed to pulse through the walls themselves. Bright lights and colorful advertisements beckoned from every direction, promising endless entertainment and adventure.

The flight had been smooth, without a hint of turbulence, and we had even managed to enjoy a drink or two while in the air, leaving us feeling lighter and more relaxed. By the time the wheels touched down and we finally landed, my anticipation was through the roof. I could not wait for the weekend to begin officially, and for that very first round of fun we had all been looking forward to.

Victoria, Anastasia, and I made our way through the terminal, our suitcases trailing behind us as we chatted animatedly. Our excitement was palpable. We were finally here, ready to celebrate Victoria's birthday and immerse ourselves in everything Vegas had to offer.

As our cab pulled up to The Cosmopolitan, I marvelled at the sleek, modern façade of the hotel. It stood tall and proud on the Strip, its glass exterior reflecting the city's dazzling lights. Inside, the lobby was a symphony of luxury and style. Crystal chandeliers hung from the ceiling, casting a soft, glittering light over the marble floors. Elegant sculptures and contemporary artwork adorned the space, adding to the hotel's chic, sophisticated atmosphere.

We checked in and made our way to our room, our excitement bubbling over as we took in the plush surroundings. The room was nothing short of spectacular. Floor-to-ceiling windows offered a breathtaking view of the Strip below, a sea of neon lights and towering buildings stretching as far as the eye could see. The decor was modern and elegant, with sleek furniture and rich fabrics that added a touch of opulence.

No matter how much my eyes wandered around, I still could not comprehend the fact that this was our reality for the rest of the weekend. Vacations were not a frequent occurrence in my life, let alone in a place like this.

"Can you believe this place?" Victoria exclaimed, her eyes wide with delight as she flopped onto one of the beds. "It's like a dream come true!"

Anastasia laughed, tossing her suitcase onto the other bed. "It's perfect. I can't wait to see what else this city has in store for us."

"So, what do you girls want to do first?" I asked, sinking into the softest mattress I had ever laid on. The longer I sat there, the more certain I felt that taking this weekend for ourselves had been the right decision. The girls were right. This was precisely what we all needed.

"I think we should hit the pools first," Anastasia suggested, fanning herself lightly with her hand. "It's pretty hot, and we might as well take advantage of everything this place has to offer."

Victoria and I shared a look that confirmed we were both more than happy with that plan. Nodding, I leaned over to open my suitcase, rummaging through the neatly packed clothes until I pulled out the swimsuits I had brought along. After a brief moment of indecision, I chose the one I wanted to wear, already excited at the thought of diving into the cool water.

All three of us changed into our swimsuits and made our way to the pool deck, where a stunning oasis awaited us. The pool area was a tropical paradise, complete with lush greenery, sparkling blue water, and luxurious cabanas. Sunbathers lounged on sleek white chaise lounges, sipping on colorful cocktails as upbeat music played softly in the background.

We found the perfect spot by the pool and settled in, stretching out as the sun poured over us, warming our skin while we soaked in the lively, carefree atmosphere. After my swim, tiny drops of water still clung to me, but the heat of the sun quickly drew them away, leaving only the soft trace of coolness behind. With each passing moment, my body loosened, and every bit of tension slipped away. I couldn't remember the last time I had felt this calm, as if the world had finally slowed down just for me.

"This is heaven," I said, stretching out on my lounge chair. "I could get used to this."

Victoria grinned, handing me a piña colada, which I gladly accepted. "Cheers to a fabulous weekend, ladies.

Tonight, we're dining at Release, and it's going to be amazing."

From what she had told us, this was one of the hottest restaurants in Vegas, known for its stunning decor and delectable seafood. Victoria had managed to snag us a reservation, and the anticipation was evident between all three of us.

"How did you manage to get that reservation? Do you have some superpower we don't know about?" Anastasia asked, raising an eyebrow with a mischievous glint.

Victoria could not hold back the laugh that slipped out of her lips. "A lady doesn't kiss and tell, surely you know that by now," she said, flashing a slight, confident smirk that made both of us grin. "I just want us to have fun, that's all."

I peeked at her from behind my sunglasses, a hint of nervousness in my voice. "I am almost scared to ask what that entails ..."

Victoria laughed again, playful and light, and gave me a gentle slap on the shoulder. "Stop it, babe. Nothing too risky. Just a healthy dose of fun. Exactly what you need." For once, I had no choice but to trust her.

As the sun began to set, casting a golden glow over the city, we headed back to our room to get ready. Victoria pulled out all of the dresses she had brought with her—all twelve of them—and went through them until she found a shimmering silver dress.

I stood in front of my open suitcase, unsure what to wear. After a long moment of hesitation, I reached for one of the safer options, a dress I had worn a handful of times before. It was simple, comfortable, and most importantly, familiar. But the moment my fingers brushed the fabric, Victoria's sharp voice echoed through the air.

"Absolutely not. Are you insane?" she said, shaking her head with exaggerated disapproval.

I blinked at her, caught off guard. "What? It's fine," I started to say, already reaching to pull out some of my other options to prove my point. Before I could, Victoria was already knee-deep in her own pile of dresses, tossing hangers aside until she pulled out a striking deep blue number. Without hesitation, she shoved it into my hands.

I held it up, staring at the dress for a long moment, my brow arching in doubt. "This is revealing," I pointed out.

Both Anastasia and Victoria turned their heads at the same time, their eyes narrowing in perfect unison, as though they were ready to battle my resistance.

"You're hot. Show off a little, girl," Victoria declared, shaking her head as if I had completely lost my mind. "All you wear are blouses and pants. And that one dress that looks like it was made for a six-year-old's birthday party. Don't even try to deny it. I've seen pictures. You've worn it every time you've gone to Sophie's friends' parties."

Heat crept to my cheeks. I wanted to argue and fire back with a witty protest, but she wasn't wrong. I *had* worn that dress more times than I wanted to admit. My mouth opened, but no words came out. Instead, I swallowed, gave a slight, reluctant nod, and retreated toward the bathroom with the dress in hand.

Slipping it on, I caught my reflection in the mirror, and for a moment I just stood there. Victoria had been right. The dress clung to me in all the right places, hugging curves I usually tried to hide. It had been so long since I wore anything like this, and yet, as I adjusted the straps and let out a small breath, I could not deny the truth. I felt good. Confident, even, as I stared at a version of myself, I had almost forgotten existed.

As I exited the bathroom, Victoria whistled at the sight. "I knew that was the right choice," she commented, and I could not help but smile. I spotted Anastasia in the corner. She had opted for a classic black cocktail dress, which highlighted her elegance. We took a moment to admire each other before heading out.

As we stepped into the elevator, Victoria turned toward us. "Let's make tonight unforgettable," she said, giving us yet another one of her signature looks. I had seen that look on her face countless times back in our university days, usually right before she talked us into doing something completely outrageous. I thought those days were long behind us. Apparently, I was wrong.

"We're not doing anything crazy, Victoria," I said firmly, though I did not miss the way the corners of her lips curved upward in that mischievous smile of hers. For a second, I almost rolled my eyes, tempted to call her out, but instead I bit back the reaction and chose to keep quiet, knowing it would not stop her either way.

We made our way to the restaurant, the neon lights of the Strip illuminating our path. The restaurant was even more breathtaking than we had imagined, with its lush greenery, twinkling lights, and chic, modern décor. Dinner at Release was an experience in itself.

The waiter greeted us the moment we walked through the door, and somehow, Victoria worked her usual magic. Within minutes, we were led to one of the best tables in the restaurant, perfectly placed with a breathtaking view spread out before us.

We slid into our seats, instantly falling into the kind of conversation that always seemed endless when the three of us were together—stories, laughter, and little updates tumbling over one another without pause. Before long, that chatter turned into the far more difficult task of deciding what to order. With so many tempting options on the menu, it felt like an impossible choice, but somehow, even that felt fun with them by my side.

The food, unsurprisingly, had been nothing short of spectacular, each dish a delicious work of art that we savored between bursts of laughter and clinking glasses. As we lingered over dessert, a decadent chocolate fondue—Victoria's phone buzzed with a new message.

Her eyes lit up as she read it, and she quickly glanced at us, her smile widening. "Girls, it's our lucky night! My friend just hit us up."

"The promoter guy?" Anastasia asked, as she arched her brow.

Victoria nodded. "He's got us a VIP section at a club where Jess Low is DJing tonight. Free bottle service and everything!" Jess Low was one of the best DJs that techno music had to offer.

Anastasia and I exchanged excited looks.

"Are you serious?" I asked, my heart racing with anticipation. It seemed that Victoria was right. This night would be unforgettable.

"Absolutely," Victoria replied, practically bouncing in her seat. She lowered her eyes to her phone, her fingers moving quickly across the screen as she typed out a message.

A moment later, she looked back up at us. "We'll have to head out soon, though. We don't want to miss this."

With our night at the restaurant coming to an end, we paid the bill and made our way back to the hotel to freshen up.

"We need new outfits," Victoria declared, as though it were a matter of life and death. I glanced down at the dress I was already wearing, which seemed more than good enough to carry me through whatever party she had in mind. But clearly, she thought otherwise.

With a soft sigh, I gave in, raising my hands in defeat. "Okay, tell me, what do you want me to wear?"

Her grin widened instantly, like she had been waiting for me to ask that very question. She dove into her suitcase, rummaging through the hangers and folded fabrics until she pulled out one of the shortest black dresses I had ever seen. My eyes widened at the sight of it, and the thought of squeezing myself into it was almost laughable. I knew better than to argue with Victoria when she got that look in her eye, though. If she suggested it, she had her reasons.

As always, she was right. The moment I slipped it on and caught my reflection in the mirror; my confidence shot through the roof. The fabric hugged me in all the right places, accentuating curves I often forgot I even had—and that happened two times tonight. Somehow, it looked even better than the blue dress, and if there was ever a moment, I felt like the truest version of myself, it was standing there in that black dress. I paired it with a simple set of black heels—nothing too flashy, but the combination worked like magic.

For the first time in a long time, I didn't just look put together ... I felt unstoppable.

Victoria settled on a glittering gold mini dress that shimmered with every movement, and Anastasia chose a sleek red dress that highlighted her graceful elegance. With one last touch of lipstick and a spritz of sexy perfume, we were ready to conquer the night.

"Okay, listen, you two," Victoria said the moment we slid into the cab, her tone suddenly shifting into something that sounded like a coach giving a pep talk before a big game. She sat forward, hands folded on her lap, her expression serious as her eyes darted between Anastasia and me. "I expect both of you to keep your eyes open tonight. There will be a bunch of cute guys at this party, and I fully expect you to utilize the chance."

Anastasia let out a soft laugh, shaking her head, while I raised a brow at her choice of words. Victoria, of course, did not so much as blink. She was dead serious.

"I thought we were here to celebrate your birthday, are we not?" I raised a brow at my best friend, confusion written all over my face.

Victoria smirked, flipping her hair as if she had just been waiting for that question. "There is absolutely no better way to honor me than by making out with a cute guy, girl. Surely you already knew that …" Her voice was light and teasing, but her eyes sparkled with mischief.

Before I could argue or roll my eyes, the car slowed to a stop in front of the club. That was the end of our conversation. We climbed out quickly, the cool night air brushing against my skin as I straightened my dress and looked up.

The place was massive, glowing with neon lights that raced along the edges of the building in shifting colors. The bass from the speakers inside was so strong I could feel it rumbling through the sidewalk. A crowd stretched down the block, a long, impatient line of people waiting for their turn to step through the doors. Luckily, waiting in line was not something we had to worry about tonight. Victoria's VIP passes had saved us countless times in the past, and tonight was no different.

"I hope you girls realize this is one of the most iconic clubs in the city," Victoria announced proudly as she guided us toward the separate VIP entrance. Even that line was busy, though it moved much faster than the regular one. She glanced back at us, her lips curved into that little smile she always wore when she was up to something. "So, when I say I want you to make the most of tonight, I mean it. If you want to meet someone fun, this is the place where you will get that."

Despite her words, I found it difficult to imagine myself meeting someone tonight. I was a mom, after all, and while I enjoyed the idea of spending the weekend with my best friends, the thought of clicking with someone to the point where I would want even to kiss them was terrifying.

That will not happen tonight, I decided, relaxing a little as my decision sank into my mind.

Inside, heat and music wrapped around me at once. The dance floor was overflowing, a restless sea of bodies swaying, jumping, and spinning to the rhythm. Lights cut through the darkness, flashing across strangers' faces, and the air was filled with energy that was unlike any other I had ever experienced.

We pushed our way through the endless sea of people, bodies brushing against us from every direction. The music was so loud it seemed to vibrate through my chest as Victoria led the way. I trailed after her with Anastasia, trying not to lose sight of her in the chaos of flashing lights and moving figures.

At last, we arrived at the **VIP** table section. The space was slightly elevated, affording it a clear view of the dance floor, and the atmosphere felt different—more exclusive, as if the air itself was lighter here. Waiting for us was a tall man with neatly styled brown hair; his posture was relaxed, but his eyes fixed on Victoria the moment he saw her. A grin spread across his face as he lifted a hand and waved her over.

"Welcome to your **VIP** section, ladies," he said with a smile, gesturing to a plush area complete with a private table and a bottle of premium vodka waiting for us. "Enjoy the night. Jess Low goes on in an hour. I've got to go now, but if you need anything else, do not hesitate to let me know."

With a slight giggle, Victoria latched onto our hands and tugged us forward, weaving us straight to our table. The second we sat down, she had already reached for the bottle. She poured each of us a shot without hesitation, sliding the glasses across the table before lifting her own.

The three of us clinked them together, but the sharp sound of glass meeting glass was lost in the thundering bass, and then we tilted our heads back in unison. The liquid burned its way down, and almost instantly, laughter burst out of us.

"To the Three Musketeers!" Anastasia announced, holding her empty glass high with a triumphant grin.

I could not help but laugh harder, shaking my head at her timing. "Wasn't that supposed to come before the shot?" I teased, nudging her playfully.

She chuckled, shoulders lifting in a little shrug, her cheeks already flushed from the warmth of the drink. "Well, we downed it before I had the chance to say anything …" she admitted with a sheepish smile.

Victoria scooped up our glasses and refilled them right away. "Do not you worry, girls. There's a simple remedy for that."

That second round was the true beginning of the night. The music seemed louder, the lights brighter, and our laughter freer. Before long, we were pulled onto the dance floor, moving together like we were the only ones in the club. Song after song blurred into one endless rhythm until finally, the crowd erupted, and we knew it was Jess Low's turn. The lights flashed in sync with the music, casting a kaleidoscope of colors across the room.

We were completely swept away by the energy that I had thought we had outgrown and left tucked away in the past. Yet here it was again, rushing back to us as if no time had passed at all. It amazed me how easily we could tap into it as though the years in between had never even existed.

Victoria pulled us both into a tight hug.

"I love you girls," she shouted over the music. "This is the best birthday weekend ever!"

"We love you too!" I shouted back, raising the half-empty glass that I somehow still managed to hold in my hand. "Here's to many more nights like this!" As the night wore on, we returned to our VIP section for more drinks and moments of respite. The bottle service was flowing, and we indulged in the luxury, reveling in the feeling of being VIPs in one of the city's hottest clubs. Even amidst all the chaos and loud music, deep down, something told me that this was only the beginning.

Four
Amelia

The next morning, I groaned as I stretched, feeling the familiar but manageable throb of a hangover. With a loud groan, I rolled onto the other side of the bed, dragging a pillow over my head in a desperate attempt to block out the world. My temples throbbed with that dull ache that only comes from one too many shots, and I squeezed my eyes shut, trying to piece myself back together. I did not even know what time it was, but the heavy glow of sunlight spilling across the room told me it was already late morning—maybe even closer to noon. The curtains had been pulled open wide, letting the sun pour in, warm and relentless against my skin.

With another grunt, I pushed myself up just enough to glance down at my attire. My dress clung to me in a wrinkled mess, and the straps were twisted—proof that I had not even managed to change last night. I remembered only bits and pieces: the sound of our giggles echoing down the hallway, Victoria leaning on Anastasia's shoulder as we stumbled inside, and then the instant blackout the moment my head hit the pillow.

Even now, the thought of standing felt like a challenge. My body begged to sink back into the mattress, but slowly, I nudged the pillow away from my face and forced myself to take in the room around me. The sunlight illuminated everything, from the discarded heels kicked into a corner to the half-empty water bottle on the nightstand.

Unsurprisingly, Victoria was already up, padding around the room in her robe, with a cup of coffee in hand. She looked surprisingly fresh, her eyes bright with lingering excitement from our incredible night out. She was already on her phone, doing God knew what, but it looked like her day had started a while ago. Anastasia stirred next to me, yawning as she propped herself up on one elbow. A glance around was all it took for me to realize the truth—I was easily in the worst shape out of the three of us.

"Morning, ladies," Victoria chirped, a hint of mischief in her voice. "How are we feeling?"

"Half-dead, I suppose," I replied, rubbing my temples. Now that I was adjusting to the sunlight in the room, though, it was getting a little easier to deal with the slight headache— so much so that I was starting to suspect there might be a cure for it after all. "Nothing some coffee and food can't fix."

Anastasia nodded in agreement. "Same here. Last night was amazing. I can't believe we actually saw Jess Low."

"Wait until you hear what's next," Victoria said, her eyes sparkling as she dragged her gaze away from the phone and right onto the two of us. "I just got a text from Jake. He's inviting us to a day party at Encore Beach Club. Bad B is DJing, and it's supposed to be the hottest pool party of the weekend."

"Bad B?" I said, my eyes widening. Sure, a weekend in Vegas sounded incredible, but I didn't expect to see so many celebrities around. "That's incredible! I've always wanted to see him live."

"I know," Victoria shrugged, taking another sip of coffee before she placed her mug down and hopped onto the bed with us. "That's exactly *why* I figured we should go. What do you say, Stasia?"

"I'm in," Anastasia said without hesitation, a smile spreading across her lips. "But first, we need food. I'm starving."

My stomach gave a loud, pitiful grumble in response. I couldn't have agreed more with its demand. Just hearing the mention of another one of my favorite DJs seemed to ease the pounding in my head, if only a little, and that tiny relief was enough to push me into motion. Slowly but surely, I started getting ready alongside the girls. For brunch, I settled on a simple white linen set, since my brain refused to cooperate when it came to piecing together anything more stylish. Coherent fashion choices were far beyond my capabilities at the moment.

Once we were all dressed, we made our way downstairs to the hotel's restaurant, the three of us chatting about what we might wear later tonight. Our conversation, however , was quickly cut short the moment the buffet table came into view.

It was impossible not to stop and stare. The hotel's buffet stretched on, an endless spread that seemed to cover every craving imaginable. Trays of fresh fruit and golden pastries stood beside steaming pans of savory dishes. A chef flipped fluffy omelets to order, filling the air with the warm scent of butter and herbs, while just a few feet away, a counter displayed delicate rolls of sushi arranged like pieces of art. My stomach grumbled once more, and then Victoria yanked us forward, prompting us to move.

We did not waste time. Plates in hand, we filled them generously, letting our eyes and appetites guide us until we could barely balance everything. Finally, we found a cozy table tucked by the wide windows, where the sunlight streamed through and wrapped us in gentle warmth. It felt like the perfect little corner to recover from last night's chaos, laugh over our fuzzy memories, and to fuel up for whatever the day ahead might throw our way.

"This place is amazing," Anastasia said, savoring a bite of her smoked salmon bagel. "I could get used to this."

"Agreed," I said, sipping my freshly squeezed orange juice. I missed Sophie more than I could put into words, but the texts from my mom—one late last night and another first thing this morning—helped ease that ache. She assured me that Sophie was doing wonderfully, happily soaking up her grandparents' attention and barely noticing that I was gone. That reassurance allowed me to relax, if only a little, and breathe without quite as much guilt.

Moreover, it made me think. Maybe it was not such a terrible thing for me to take a weekend here and there for myself, especially now that Sophie was growing older, braver, and a little more independent each day. She had her own little world to enjoy, and time with her grandparents was part of that. For me, it meant moments like this, where I could laugh with my best friends and remember the version of myself that existed before the responsibilities of marketing deadlines and motherhood consumed every corner of my life.

"I'm so glad we decided to do this trip. It's exactly what we needed. Thank you for talking me into doing this," I continued, and the words barely scratched the gratitude I felt at that moment.

Anastasia arched a perfectly shaped brow. "Does that mean we might actually convince you to take more trips like this?"

Her question made me laugh under my breath, and though I tried to play it off, I could not stop the smile tugging at my lips. "Maybe …" I admitted, dragging the word out just enough to keep them guessing.

That was all it took. Both of my best friends squealed like excited schoolgirls, clapping their hands together in delight as if they had already started planning the next getaway in their heads. I shook my head, fighting the urge to roll my eyes.

We carried on with our brunch, nibbling between laughs and half-serious conversations about outfits for the night ahead. Just as I was about to grab us some dessert, the sharp vibration of Victoria's phone against the table cut through the moment.

She picked it up, and her face brightened right away. "Alright, girls, I've just been informed that the day party starts at noon, and Jake has already secured us a prime spot. Let's finish up here and get ready to soak up some sun and dance to Bad B."

Both Anastasia and I loved the idea, even if my head did slightly protest at the thought of being out in the sun, but that was quickly overshadowed by the excitement of choosing what we were going to wear. This time, Victoria opted for a stylish red bikini with gold accents, Stas chose a sleek black one-piece that highlighted her graceful figure, and I went for a vibrant turquoise bikini that made me feel confident and ready for another day of fun. It had been a long time since I last allowed myself to show my body like that, but I could not deny that it felt good.

With sunglasses, heels, and sun hats in tow, we made our way to Encore Beach Club. The atmosphere was electric as we approached, and the music grew louder with each step. Any other time, this would have been the last place I'd want to be. Usually, would have booked a family-friendly hotel, the kind with a shallow pool where Sophie could splash around while I lounged nearby, mocktail in hand, always keeping one eye on her. But this time was different. There were no responsibilities, no routine, and no little voice calling for me every few minutes. I could fully focus on myself and my friends.

The pool area looked like something out of a resort magazine. Towering palm trees swayed gently in the breeze, their shadows rippling across rows of white lounge chairs. Sleek cabanas, draped with flowing white curtains, offered little pockets of shade, while the pool itself stretched out like a glittering mirror, so big it seemed endless. The place was overflowing with energy—music thumping, laughter echoing, and people dancing at the water's edge. Everywhere I turned, there were cocktails in neon colors, trays of shots being passed around, and the sharp smell of alcohol mixing with the sweetness of sunscreen.

I couldn't even imagine touching a drink right now; just the thought of it made my stomach turn. What I wanted instead was simple—sun on my skin, the company of my friends, and a few carefree hours to enjoy it all.

It didn't take long before Jake appeared, weaving through the crowd with an apologetic smile tugging at his lips. He ran a hand through his short, brown hair.

"Hey, ladies. I hope you're enjoying yourselves," he said.

Victoria gave a quick nod, and a broad smile spread across her face. "Hell yes, we are. We can't thank you enough for everything you've done for us so far."

Jake shifted a little, as if that thought made him uneasy. "Yeah, hold that thought. I don't know how to say this, but well, I've got a bit of a dilemma. The table I secured for you has been double-booked."

My heart dipped for just a moment, though I reminded myself it was not the end of the world. There was still plenty to enjoy—the warm sun soaking into my skin, the endless stream of drinks, and the laughter that came with being surrounded by my best friends. I could have settled into all of that without a single complaint.

Victoria, though, I was not so sure she'd feel the same. She slid her sunglasses up to the top of her head. Her lips parted, but before she could get a word out, Jake quickly continued, "But I've got a backup plan. There's a group of soccer players with a cabana, and they could use a few beautiful women like yourselves to make the cabana look more fun. Give me a minute."

Neither of us had a chance to process it, let alone respond, before he was already moving away. Our eyes followed him as he crossed the pool deck, heading toward a man stretched out on a lounge chair. He wore simple shorts and a basic white tee; gold sunglasses perched on his nose. After a brief conversation, Jake returned with the man in tow.

"Ladies, this is Julian," Jake introduced. Now that he was closer, we finally got a proper look at him. He was tall, his frame easy to notice even in the crowded space, with skin bronzed from the sun and dark hair that caught the light when he moved. A small smile curved his lips as his gaze swept over the three of us. "He's the event coordinator for the team."

Julian smiled warmly at us. "How many of you are joining us?"

"It's just the three of us," Victoria replied.

"Stunning," Julian said, his smile widening. "Come, follow me."

We exchanged glances that contained a mix of excitement and suspicion, but decided to follow him. Julian led us to an elite VIP section—a cabana overlooking the entire party. It was decked out with its own private pool, plush seating, and an array of drinks.

"All the drinks are on us, of course," he said, his hand sweeping toward the bar set up at the back of the cabana. The cabana itself was breathtaking, easily twice the size of any of the others, with flowing curtains, deep cushioned seats, and a view that made the whole pool feel like it belonged to us. It was hard to believe we were really here, sitting in the middle of it all, and harder still to think that, for once, we were the ones being treated this way.

"We also keep a security guard nearby, just to keep an eye on the party," he added casually. "Most of the time we don't need him, but people tend to feel more at ease knowing he's there."

Whatever suspicions we had carried with us earlier dissolved right then. The whole setup felt safe, almost natural, and Jake's offer no longer seemed the least bit strange. The mix-up with the double-booked table was already long forgotten.

"Anything you need, just let me know," Julian said, though his attention was already drifting toward someone across the cabana. "Now, if you'll excuse me, I'll have to step away, but please, enjoy yourselves, ladies. We're happy to have you here."

As soon as he disappeared into the crowd, Victoria whipped toward us, her face lighting up with the biggest grin. Her eyes swept over the cabana, taking in the scene around us—tall, athletic men lounging with drinks in hand.

Hooking her arms through ours, Victoria leaned in with a conspiratorial look. "This could not have worked out any better for us. I told you we'd meet some guys on this trip," she murmured.

I could not stop the laugh that slipped out, though it held more exasperation than amusement. "No, you were *hoping* for it, Vic. But I told you, I'm here to celebrate your birthday, not hook up with someone."

The idea alone made my chest tighten. The thought of putting myself out there again felt impossible. Brad's absence was a scar that still throbbed whenever I thought about letting someone in. And even if I wanted to, what would be the point? I was only here for the weekend. Quick flings had never been my style, and I did not see that changing now.

One of the players broke away from the group and headed toward us. He was tall, with a smile so easy it was impossible not to be drawn to it. His skin was a deep, warm brown that glowed under the cabana lights, and his dark curls framed his facial features. When his brown eyes landed on us, there was a spark of curiosity there.

"Hey, I'm Taije," he introduced himself. "We just won the league championship. Care to join us for a celebratory shot?"

"Straight to the point," Victoria teased, earning a laugh from all of us. "I like that."

"A man has to shoot his shot with pretty ladies like yourselves," he retorted jokingly, with a wide smile.

"What team do you play for?" I asked, intrigued.

"We're with Miami Wave FC," Taije replied proudly, slinging his hands into his pockets. "Just clinched the league title last week."

"Congratulations!" Anastasia said with a slight nod. "That's amazing!"

"It is. Still feels surreal," Taije said, giving us a long, easy look before flashing that charming smile again. "Why don't I grab you girls some cocktails? You can't just stand here empty-handed …"

The idea should've excited me, but my stomach turned at the thought of drinking again. Still, the trays being carried around were far too tempting to ignore. Cocktails in every color imaginable caught my attention—served in tall, frosted glasses, short crystal tumblers, and even delicate flutes. Each one was dressed up with little umbrellas, sugared rims, slices of fruit, or sprigs of herbs. They looked like candy in liquid form, completely irresistible.

In the end, the three of us exchanged a glance and gave a slight nod.

"What should I bring you?" he asked, leaning in slightly.

"Just surprise us," Victoria said with a playful smirk. "Get us something *you* think we'll like."

My brows arched. Was she flirting with him? Very possible. It was exactly her style. Taije's smile deepened, and with a quick nod, he turned toward the bar where the bartender was already hard at work shaking and pouring.

"He's cute, isn't he?" Anastasia murmured, bumping her shoulder against Victoria's. I couldn't help smiling, too.

"I suppose so," Victoria admitted with a little shrug, though the glint in her eye betrayed her. "But let's not get carried away. Who knows where the night will take us ..."

It wasn't long before Taije returned, balancing a whiskey for himself and three pale pink cocktails, each one topped with fresh mint and a pair of raspberries.

We clinked our glasses together, laughter bubbling between us.

"To new friends in places like this!" Victoria toasted.

"And to the champions, of course!" I added, lifting my glass a little higher. "Thank you for the drinks." Our drinks touched, and then we each took a sip. The taste was sweet refreshing, and it hit my tongue just right.

The beats of Bad B's music pounded through the air, vibrating against the backdrop of laughter and splashing water. The day party at Encore Beach Club was in full swing, and we were right in the heart of it, celebrating with the Miami Wave FC soccer team. Players came and went, introducing themselves and making a small, pleasant chat, but never lingering for too long. And that was just how I preferred it. I liked that it was not too overwhelming or too forward, and found myself relaxing more than I expected. Shots and cocktails flowed freely, and the sun beat down relentlessly, making the pool water feel like a refreshing escape.

Once the alcohol kicked in, the initial nervousness I felt around the soccer players dissolved into an easy camaraderie. We danced with them, chatted, and exchanged stories as if we'd known each other for years. Victoria and Anastasia were deep in conversation with some of the other players, while I found myself roaming around, everywhere and nowhere, all at once.

No matter how much I shifted or turned, I couldn't shake the feeling that someone was watching me, constantly. And, of course, I wasn't imagining it.

When I finally turned around, the first thing I noticed was his dark, tousled hair falling effortlessly over his forehead, giving him that perfect mix of rugged and stylish. Then came his eyes, deep, dark brown, sharp, and confident, making it impossible to look away.

His presence was magnetic. Broad shoulders, toned arms, and an athletic frame that spoke of years spent training for soccer made him impossible to ignore. Every feature seemed carefully sculpted—the strong jawline, the high cheekbones, and that smile was capable of lighting up the entire space. I felt a flutter of butterflies rising in my stomach immediately, impossible to ignore. Then I realized—he was staring right at me. *Right at me.*

And he smiled.

It felt as if all the air had been knocked out of my lungs right at that moment in the best way possible. My knees buckled for a brief moment as I tried to keep my composure. Never in a million years did I think a guy like that would look at me. In fact, I did not even think I would've ever notice it, but I did, and we made eye contact, and now this encounter felt impossible to escape. The only question was, who would make the first move?

The smile on my lips lingered just long enough to send the signal. I wanted him to come over. He caught on quickly. With an easy stride and his hands tucked casually into his pockets, he made his way toward me.

Up close, he was even more striking. The details that had stood out from a distance, his jawline, his eyes, and that disarming smile—felt magnified now, impossible to ignore. When that smile flickered across his face again, my heart skipped.

"Hey," he said as he leaned casually against the table beside me.

"Hey," I replied, suddenly all too aware of the heat creeping into my cheeks. My chest tightened with nerves. When was the last time I had even tried something like this? Not since Brad. Back then, dating felt new and exciting, but after he left, I had built walls around myself so high that even when other men asked me out, I never let it go anywhere.

Now, standing here with his steady eyes locked on mine, I felt a pressure to say something before the silence stretched too long. The first words tumbled out before I could stop them. "I'm Amelia James."

"Diego Alvarez," he replied, extending his hand toward me. I shook it firmly, my insides tingling even at that slight touch.

"Diego," I repeated, testing the name on my tongue. "Nice to meet you."

"I have to admit, that my eyes have been on you from the moment I first spotted you," he admitted, and my breath caught in the back of my throat. The openness of his approach left me weak in my knees.

I brushed a strand of my hair out of my face. "Is that so?" I teased, a playful grin spreading across my lips.

Diego chuckled, and the sound struck me right at the heart. "Guilty as charged, or sin since we are in Vegas. Can you blame me?"

I was unable to help the laugh that soon escaped my lips. "I guess not. So, Diego, what's your story?"

He gestured for me to sit down next to him, and I obliged, settling in comfortably with my cocktail in hand. "I'm a defender for Miami Wave FC. We just won the league championship, as you may have heard, hence the celebration."

"So, I've heard," I nodded, "and I suppose congratulations are in order, then."

His smile widened, and for a moment it felt almost impossible to tear my eyes away. There was something magnetic about the way his gaze softened ever so slightly as it locked with mine, as if he were seeing straight through me.

I had promised myself I wasn't interested in this anymore. Dating, flirting, even casual conversations with men all felt like a distraction from what really mattered. My focus had to stay on Sophie, on giving her the best life I could and building a career that would provide us both with security.

Still, standing there with him, things began shifting inside my head. I started wondering what harm could come from enjoying the thrill of being noticed, of wanting and being wanted in return? The thought surprised me, yet it lingered, tugging at me with a temptation I hadn't allowed myself in so long.

Before I could stop it, the question whispered through my mind: would it really be so wrong if tonight ended with more than just conversation, if it ended with his lips on mine?

Diego's voice snapped me back into reality, and my gaze locked onto his once more.

"Thanks. And what about you? What brings you to Vegas?"

"We're here for a girls' trip," I explained, gesturing toward where Victoria and Anastasia were laughing with some of his teammates. "Celebrating a friend's birthday."

"Ah, the infamous birthday celebrations in Vegas," Diego said, nodding knowingly. "I've heard stories. Is this your first time here?"

"Well, we're living them, and yes, it's my first time here," I said with a laugh. "It's been fun so far, though I'll admit it's been a long while since I've been hungover. My friends and I go way back to our university days, and I honestly thought parties like this were behind us. But when Victoria suggested we do this …" I let the words trail off, realizing I was rambling. Grateful for the distraction, I tipped back the last sip of my drink, the sweetness clinging to my tongue as I swallowed. "I couldn't say no."

"That doesn't surprise me," Diego said. He gave a slight shrug. "I think all of us should have our time to relax and let go once in a while." His gaze flicked to the empty glass still lingering in my hand, then back up to meet my eyes. A small, knowing smile curved his lips. "Can I get you another drink?"

"Sure." I nodded, though out of the corner of my eye I caught Victoria and Anastasia watching me like hawks. Heat rushed to my cheeks again, and I tried to mask it. The effort completely crumbled the moment I locked eyes with Victoria. She gave me an exaggerated grin, flashing two thumbs up and raising her brows in a way that made her intentions *very* clear.

My mouth fell open in shock, and I quickly tore my gaze away, praying Diego had not noticed. Luckily, he had already flagged down a passing server as he ordered a cocktail for me and a whiskey for himself.

"I hope it's all right that I took it upon myself to order for you," he said politely, observing me with those brown eyes that somehow made the rest of the world vanish around us. "Everyone keeps raving about this cocktail, and I figured you might like it …" His words trailed off, and almost immediately he added, "But of course, if you don't, I can get you something else."

"No, no," I said quickly, shaking my head. "That's absolutely fine. Honestly, the cocktails here have been a massive hit. I've loved every single one I've tried."

The reassurance seemed to settle him. His shoulders eased ever so slightly, and the tension in his expression softened into that warm smile again.

"So, how's the athlete life treating you? It must be exciting. You get to travel all over the world, play in massive stadiums, and then end up at parties like this …" I asked softly, thanking him with a slight nod as I accepted the drink he had ordered for me.

The martini glass felt cool in my hand, and when I brought it to my lips, the blue liquid hit my tongue with a surprising mix of sweet and sour. Normally it wouldn't have been my first choice, but tonight, I didn't mind it at all. In fact, maybe I liked it even more because Diego was watching me so intently, his dark eyes studying my reaction as though my opinion mattered more than anything else at that moment. I offered him a small smile of approval, and only then did he lift his own glass and take a slow sip of his whiskey.

"It can be a lot of work," he admitted, setting his glass back down with ease. "Especially during the season. We have multiple training sessions a day, constant travel, and endless pressure. But I can't complain. I love what I do. And parties like this," he gestured loosely around the cabana, "are a massive plus. Especially when I get to meet women like you. Though …" his lips curved into a smile, "I can't say I've ever met anyone quite like you before."

A laugh slipped out of me before I could stop it, light and incredulous. My heart gave an unsteady skip, but I did my best to hold my composure. "You've only known me for, what, a few minutes?" I teased, arching a brow at him. "How could you possibly know what I'm like?"

Diego didn't flinch at the challenge. If anything, his smile softened. "True," he said smoothly. "But I've been watching you for a little while. Ever since you walked in, actually, I couldn't take my eyes off you. There was something about your smile … I knew I had to come over, one way or another." He gave a slight shrug, almost sheepish, though the way his eyes lingered on me made the air between us feel charged. The whole thing felt like something pulled straight out of a rom-com, something I never thought I'd actually live. "This isn't my usual approach, either," he added quietly, as though letting me in on a secret.

Now he had my full attention. I tilted my head slightly, curiosity slipping into my voice. "Oh? And what is your usual approach?"

"It doesn't matter," he said with a teasing grin, "as long as this one is working."

That earned him a small smile from me, though nerves twisted in my stomach. "In that case, I should probably admit something too," I confessed, the words tumbling out before I could stop them. "I don't usually let myself surrender to the moment like this. I have trouble letting people approach me, but you've caught my eye."

The second the words left my lips, my chest tightened. Had I really just admitted that? To him? Heat rushed through me, and my heartbeat thundered so loudly it became a ringing in my ears. It was all I could hear.

"Then tell me more about you," Diego said, leaning in ever so slightly. His voice was warm and steady. "You seem to have me at a disadvantage. You already know more about me than I do about you."

I laughed, shaking off some of the tension. "There isn't much to say, I suppose. I live in Houston, and I'm a Marketing Director. I've been in my role for five years now. It's hardly as glamorous as your career, but I do love what I do."

For a brief second, I considered mentioning Sophie, the most important part of my life, but this moment wasn't meant for that kind of vulnerability. This was just conversation, something fleeting only for tonight, so I kept it to myself.

"Trust me," Diego said with a nudge, his grin easy and sure. "Behind every good athlete, there's a marketing team working overtime. Don't underestimate yourself. Image is everything, but I bet you already know that."

He wasn't wrong. In the world we lived in, reputation could make you or break you. The public could crown you in one breath and tear you apart in the next.

"And that's why our manager likes to keep parties like these pretty tame," he added, that smile of his returning like a weapon aimed straight at my heartbeat.

"You call this tame?" I asked, scrunching my face in disbelief as I glanced around.

The scene spoke for itself—people were spilling onto the dance floor, drinks sloshing in their hands, laughter and shouts rising above the thumping bass that poured from the massive speakers. The whole place shimmered under the late-afternoon sun, which dipped lower by the minute.

Somewhere out there, one of my favorite DJs had started his set a long time ago, but I barely noticed. For once, I wasn't chasing the excitement of the crowd. Instead, I was caught up in the moment. It wasn't long before the truth hit me. I was enjoying myself more than I had in a very long time.

"Actually, yes," Diego grinned, tilting his head to the side. "Now tell me, do you dance?" Without waiting for my answer, he stood up and extended his hand to me.

"I love to dance," I replied. That much was true, but I never imagined I would admit it out loud so easily, much less find myself about to dance with someone again. Yet before I could talk myself out of it, I slipped my hand into his and let Diego guide me toward the dance floor.

The music thumped through the speakers, fast and heavy with rhythm. It was the kind of beat that made the crowd lose themselves completely. I didn't know the steps, and honestly, I didn't care. Neither did he. Somehow, without trying, our movements found each other—our bodies swaying together as if we'd been partners on the floor for years.

What struck me most was his restraint. Around us, couples were tangled together, hands wandering, movements blurring into something far more suggestive than dancing. Still, Diego's touch stayed steady and respectful. His hands never strayed beyond the places they should be. That, more than anything, made me feel at ease and safe.

"You weren't joking," I said into his ear as I leaned closer, raising my voice just enough to be heard over the music. "With the way you dance, you really do keep yourself tame at these parties …"

His lips curved into the faintest smile before he leaned down, his breath brushing my cheek. "Sweetheart," he murmured. The single word sent a shiver rolling through me. I hadn't realized something so simple could affect me that way, but in his voice, it was almost dangerous. "When my hands end up on you, it won't be because of the dancing."

My lips parted, and I wanted to say something, but for once, I found myself at a loss for words. The music blurred after that, turning into a haze of beats and voices, but those words stayed with me, echoing in my chest. Every now and then, his gaze dipped toward my lips, lingering there just long enough to make me sure he was about to kiss me, but he didn't. To my own surprise, disappointment bloomed inside me, consuming me entirely. All I could wonder was whether he'd do it by the end of the night.

Eventually, Victoria and Anastasia found me excusing themselves as they pulled me away from Diego for a moment. I could tell they expected me to tell them *everything*, even if I knew they saw it all.

"Amelia, you've been keeping secrets!" Victoria teased, nudging me playfully. "Who's that cute guy you've been dancing with?"

I rolled my eyes. "I have *not* been keeping secrets. I just haven't had the time to tell you everything," I murmured, shaking my head, though my smile was impossible to hold back. "His name is Diego and… "

"Well, he seems smitten," Anastasia observed with a knowing smile.

"He's not smitten," I countered, arching my brow. "We've just been enjoying some time together …"

Victoria rolled her eyes playfully, repeating a motion of my own. "Are you going to see him again?"

"I hope so," I admitted, feeling a flutter of anticipation settle in my stomach.

"Go," Victoria urged, giving me a gentle push in Diego's direction. "We'll see you back at the hotel. Have fun."

I parted my lips, wanting to debate her, but it wasn't long before I decided against it. Because for the first time in a long time, this was something I *wanted*.

Five
Diego

Amelia James.

I could not recall the last time I had met someone who radiated such vibrant, beautiful energy that reached me even across the other side of the pool. Being around her at the party was unforgettable, of course, with the music shaking the ground, drinks flowing without pause, people laughing, and bodies swaying in rhythm to every beat. Yet there was a deeper part of me that longed for more than just the noise and the thrill. I wanted to sit with her, speak to her, and truly know her.

I tried not to roll my eyes at myself for even thinking this way. If those words had ever slipped from my mouth in front of my teammates, they would have mocked me relentlessly, dragging it out for weeks. Still, I could not deny what I was feeling, no matter how hard I tried to push it away. It would have been foolish, almost impossible, to convince myself otherwise.

I watched her closely as she returned from her friends, her face adorned with a smile that seemed to stretch time itself. In that moment, I knew without hesitation that smile would remain etched in my memory for as long as I lived.

"So, where to now?" she asked, her eyes lifting to meet mine.

"Let's go somewhere quieter," I replied gently, taking the lead and guiding her away from the chaos of the pool. I had spent enough nights at this hotel to know it better than most, and I was certain of a rooftop bar with a calmer atmosphere, one more suited to meaningful conversations.

We slipped through the crowd together until the music softened behind us. Inside the elevator, I pressed the final button to carry us all the way up to the rooftop.

Even in that ordinary moment, I found my eyes refusing to leave her. The elevator light reflected against her features, softening them in a way that made it even harder to look away. Amelia noticed my gaze, and the corner of her lips curled into a faint smile. She tilted her head slightly, studying me.

"What?" she asked, her eyebrow lifting.

"Nothing," I murmured, sliding my hands into my pockets, suddenly aware of the closeness between us. "I was only thinking how rare it feels to have someone like you here, beside me, in the middle of all this noise. You're so incredibly beautiful, intelligent, and well-spoken …"

Parties like these usually served one purpose only to celebrate whatever occasion called for it, whether it was a victory, a holiday, or simply an excuse to drink until the night blurred. Most girls came for the dancing, the chase, and the drinks that kept flowing without end. That was fine, because once upon a time I had been exactly like that too, careless and content with surface-level thrills. Something shifted, though, the instant my eyes caught her for the first time. It was as though the rules of the night changed, and all I wanted was more than just a blur of faces and noise.

Her cheeks warmed with a faint blush, and the sight made me smile without thinking.

"You're flattering me far too much," she murmured, shaking her head as if to dismiss the words. Before I could respond, the elevator chimed softly, the doors sliding open to reveal the rooftop bar above.

Green accents draped across the space, and tiny strings of fairy lights glowed against polished glass and sleek, modern furniture. Conversations lingered here in quiet tones, people gathered at tables with drinks in hand, leaning closer to share thoughts rather than shout over the bass pounding below. The chaos from the pool party still drifted faintly upward, but here it was only a hum in the background, softened by the breathtaking view of the Las Vegas Strip stretching before us.

I guided her toward a corner table, my hand resting lightly at her back, and she didn't stop smiling the entire way. I found myself wanting to capture it and hold onto it for the rest of the night.

The moment we settled in, a tall blonde waitress approached us and offered us a bright, professional smile, her eyes flickering between Amelia and me.

"Good evening, and welcome to Divine. I'm Tanya, and I'll be your server tonight. Do you know what you'd like to order?"

I glanced at Amelia, ready to give her more time if she needed it, but she was quicker than I was.

"I'll have an iced tea, peach flavor, please," she said softly, and then she looked at me with a small laugh in her eyes. "I've had enough to drink down at the pool, and I want to enjoy this moment the way it deserves to be enjoyed."

That small smile returned to her face, and in that instant my decision came without hesitation. I turned toward the waitress and gave a quiet nod. "Make it two, please," I instructed. Tanya acknowledged the request with a polite dip of her head before walking away to prepare our drinks. My attention, however, had already shifted back to Amelia.

"Tell me," I asked, leaning forward slightly, "how do you like your job? Is that something you always pictured yourself doing?"

Amelia paused for a moment, as though she weighed each word before allowing it to escape her lips. "I don't know," she admitted. "For a while, I worked a lot of different jobs, nothing that lasted very long, just enough to help me keep up with rent, bills, and everything else life demanded. Eventually, I found a position in marketing. It was not glamorous at first and certainly nothing to brag about, but it was stable, reliable, and surprisingly comfortable. Over time, I grew into that role, slowly realizing that I was good at it. Years passed, and little by little, I climbed higher. Now I am in a place where the work feels good. Challenging. I like it because it pushes me to think differently every day."

Tanya returned with our drinks, carefully setting them down in front of us. Amelia reached for her glass and took a slow sip of the peach iced tea. Then she looked back at me with curiosity written all over her face. "What about you? Do you enjoy what you do? Is this something you always dreamed of pursuing?"

I gave a slight shrug, a smile tugging at the corner of my mouth. "I suppose so. Soccer has been part of my life since childhood. From the moment I learned to kick a ball, I wanted to make the sport my career. It came naturally, and it felt right. My dad, of course, insisted that I finish college and have a backup plan just in case things did not work out. Still, deep down, I always knew this would be what I pursued, no matter the obstacles." A pause followed, but it was not the uncomfortable kind. "Houston, huh?" I finally said, recalling the town she had mentioned earlier. "How do you like it there?"

"Can't complain, really," Amelia replied, her smile softening. "The town is wonderful, and I've built a good life for myself there. Have you ever been to Houston?"

I shook my head slowly. "I haven't, although now I'm beginning to realize there might be a reason for me to visit, if things continue to go the way I hope they will."

Her brow lifted ever so slightly, curiosity laced through the faint smile that had been teasing me all night. "Oh? Is that so? What, exactly, would be the deciding factor for you?"

I reached forward, my hand brushing lightly against her cheek before tucking a strand of hair gently behind her ear. She shivered at the touch, and that alone was a subtle reaction that told me this closeness affected her as much as it affected me.

"I can't reveal all my secrets, sweetheart," I murmured, leaning in closer so that my words came as a whisper against her ear. Every part of me wanted to close the small gap between us and kiss her right then, yet somehow, I managed to resist. The timing did not feel quite right.

For now, at least.

The restraint seemed wise, because the conversation flowed with an ease I had never known before. She spoke about her hobbies and the marketing campaigns she had worked on, and I shared what it was like to stand beneath the spotlight, and all the pressure and the exhilaration that came with a career like mine.

As the night moved forward and the minutes slipped by unnoticed, I realized the time was nearing for the premade plans I had agreed to earlier. A part of me wanted nothing more than to abandon them altogether so I could stay there with Amelia until dawn. I knew, however, that my managers and teammates would not take kindly to that decision. Still, I hoped she might want to come with me, just so that I could spend a little more time with her.

"We're heading to a club later," I said, my eyes never leaving hers. "You should come with us."

Amelia hesitated, glancing down at our intertwined hands. Up until this point, I hadn't even realized they were somehow linked. "I'll think about it," she murmured after a brief pause, "It's Victoria's birthday, and we might have other plans."

I squeezed her hand gently. I understood that, but the more impatient and selfish part of me still wanted to see her again, if even for a little while. "I really want to see you again. The rest of our time here, I mean. Think about it, okay? Bring your friends along. It'll be fun." I paused for a moment. "Give me your phone."

"What?" Amelia let out a small, snuffed laugh, and I extended my hand toward her to show her that I meant it. Slowly, hesitantly, she reached for me and placed her phone in my hand. I quickly entered my number and sent myself a text.

"There. You have my number now, and I have yours," I said, handing it back to her. "I'll have a taxi pick you and your girls up. Just think about it."

"I'll see what the girls want to do," she promised, and I internally crossed my fingers that they were in the mood for clubbing too. I smiled, leaning in to press a soft kiss to her cheek. That was as far as I wanted to go for now.

"I hope to see you soon," was all I said as she stepped out of the elevator and unlocked her hotel room. The elevator door closed, and I was left with the hope that I would see her again.

Six
Amelia

By the time I finally stepped into my hotel room, my heart was pounding so wildly in my chest that I half expected it might break free at any moment. The heavy door clicked shut behind me, and my knees felt weak, as though they were ready to give out, still, a smile tugged at my lips despite the rush of nerves. That smile only grew stronger when my eyes landed on Victoria and Anastasia sprawled comfortably across the beds.

I hurried toward them without hesitation and flopped onto the mattress beside them, the cushions dipping beneath my weight as a burst of laughter escaped me.

"Spill it, girl," Victoria demanded, her elbow nudging me with the playful insistence that she always showed when she suspected something had happened.

"You'd better tell us everything, no holding back," Anastasia added with a grin, nodding slightly.

My cheeks flared, and I could hardly form the words resting on the tip of my tongue. My stomach fluttered with butterflies, jumbling my thoughts into incoherent sentences. The sensation was unlike anything I had known before. It felt as if I were experiencing the kind of dizzy, uncontainable excitement most people first discovered when they were seventeen… and madly into someone for the first time.

"What can I say? Diego and I spent the rest of the evening talking and getting to know each other better. We were at the rooftop bar and just talking about everything and nothing at the same time. And I have to say, it's been a while since the last time I felt this comfortable with someone," I admitted.

"Oh, my God! I knew it!" Victoria squealed. "I knew you were going to meet someone and—"

"That doesn't mean anything," I quickly said, even though I *wanted* it to mean something. Was that crazy? Possibly. But I realized that, for once, I didn't care. It had been so long since I last felt this way, and for one selfish night, I wanted to explore it.

"Sure," Victoria dragged the word out, keeping her gaze on mine, "but I have a strong feeling that's not all there is …"

I exhaled softly. "He invited us to go to a club with him and his teammates later. He even put his number in my phone and said he'd send an Uber for us."

Anastasia raised an eyebrow. "And are we going?"

"I don't know," I said honestly. "I told him I'd think about it. I want to see him again, but it's your birthday, Victoria. What do you want to do?"

Victoria pretended to be momentarily lost in thought, gently tapping her chin. For a moment, I thought she might want to hang out with just us girls, but the moment I saw the smile spread across her face, all those doubts vanished.

"You should go for it. This is Vegas. We're here to have fun, and I already told you that the best present you can give me is to get with a guy …" Victoria said at last. I rolled my eyes, and she instantly held her hands up, as if to show she meant no harm. "I mean it, though. You deserve to have some fun. That's the main reason *why* we got here anyway, isn't it?"

I arched my brow. "I thought the main reason why we got here was your birthday …"

Victoria waved me off. "That too. But still, I want you girls to have fun. Besides, cute guys in the club? Count me in. I can't complain about that." A wide grin spread across her face, and I knew we were all in.

"What are you waiting for?" Anastasia nudged me once more. "Go on, text him …"

With another small sigh, I reached for my phone, noticing how my fingers trembled ever so slightly as I began typing the words across the screen. The soft glow of the display lit my face while my friends watched me like hawks.

Me:

> Guess who … I talked to Victoria and Anastasia, and they're down to go out to the club with me. If you're still up for it, of course.

My teeth pressed against my bottom lip as I stared at the screen, my eyes locked on the message as soon as it was marked as read. A moment later, the bubble with three moving dots appeared, sending my heart into another frenzy.

Diego:

> Of course. I can't wait to see you. I'll have a taxi pick you girls up in about an hour. Does that work for you?

Me:

> Absolutely :)

Diego:

Perfect. Looking forward to
seeing you again.

The quickness of his reply made my heart pound harder as I set the phone down on the bed and glanced at them. Both Anastasia and Victoria stared at me with wide eyes, clearly waiting for me to share the result. I fought the urge to roll my eyes at their exaggerated suspense, although a small laugh escaped me all the same.

"I texted him, just like I said I would," I announced, folding my hands in my lap for a brief moment before letting them drop back to my sides. "He said he'll have a taxi pick us up in an hour."

The words were hardly out of my mouth before the two of them were nearly vibrating with excitement, making it obvious they were just as thrilled about the plans as I was.

Victoria parted her lips first, her eyes darting between Anastasia and me as though she could already see the night unfolding. "An hour?" she repeated in a low tone filled with disbelief. "Then we'd better start getting ready."

Without hesitation, she grabbed our hands and tugged us both to our feet. In her true dramatic fashion, she immediately took over, determined to make sure I looked flawless for the occasion, as though the entire night depended on it.

I ended up in a stunning red cocktail dress that hugged my curves and accentuated my figure, complete with a plunging neckline and thigh-high slit. Victoria, on the other hand, chose a glamorous gold dress that shimmered under the lights with its intricate sequins. Anastasia wore a sleek silver mini dress that draped perfectly over her toned figure, and the halter neck and backless style showed off her slender frame. This weekend had me feeling alive in a way I had not experienced in years, perhaps even longer. A spark pulsed inside me, making me look forward to going out again, despite my body's protest of exhaustion. The thrill outweighed the fatigue, so I ignored it and savored the anticipation.

The taxi ride passed in what felt like seconds, and my thoughts drifted too quickly for me to keep track of the streets outside the window. Before I knew it, the driver pulled to a stop in front of the club.

The moment I stepped out, Diego was already there, greeting me with a soft kiss on the cheek. He was dressed casually in shorts paired with a light linen button-up shirt, and the fabric clung to him just enough to reveal the definition of his body beneath. My eyes betrayed me, lingering far too long on him. The way I could not look away was almost maddening—I was in my thirties, a grown woman with years of experience behind me, yet here I was, reacting as though I were back in my early twenties, completely swept away by handsome men.

Behind him, the music pumped through the air. The bass thundered in perfect rhythm with the flashing lights that pulsed across the crowded floor. The sea of bodies moved together, as though each person were guided by an invisible thread tied to the beat of the music. The energy was overwhelming in its intensity, though I hardly noticed any of it. All of my attention was on *him*.

"I'm so glad you came," Diego murmured, his lips brushing close to my ear. That single motion was enough to send another tremor rippling through my body, no matter how desperately I tried to steady myself.

"Me too," I whispered back. My gaze flicked away from him for a brief moment, searching for my friends in the chaos. I spotted them quickly on the far side of the table, already laughing and immersed in conversation with a few of his teammates. They looked perfectly at ease, which only heightened the strange blend of emotions stirring inside me.

Diego shifted closer, his arm sliding gently around my waist. He pulled me against him until I could feel the warmth radiating from his body.

"You know," he said, "I couldn't find a way out of this party tonight. Our manager said we had to attend it, even if only for a short time. The truth is, I would rather be anywhere else , with you."

His words made my breath catch. I felt the tremble again, stronger this time, as my eyes locked with his. The intensity of his gaze seemed to unravel me in seconds, stripping me of every excuse to look away.

"Do you want to get out of here?" he asked, almost daringly.

Without hesitation, I nodded. The magnetic pull between us was impossible to resist. Diego took my hand, leading me through the throng of dancing bodies until we stepped out of the club. The air outside was cool and refreshing compared to the heat inside the club, but the fire between us burned hotter than ever.

"Did you want to go somewhere else or …"

"No," I interrupted softly, the word slipping out before I could stop it. His hand remained linked with mine as he looked down at me. "I just want to walk with you for a while."

Diego's lips lifted into a faint smile as he gave a slight nod. His hand tightened around mine, and we began moving forward at an unhurried pace. The streets were filled with people, laughter, footsteps, and the hum of late-night energy that never seemed to rest. Even so, a pocket of silence wrapped itself around us. It wasn't heavy or awkward, though, but comforting and almost magnetic.

I had no idea how long we walked like that, holding hands while the city stretched endlessly before us. At some point, an empty bench appeared just a few feet away, tucked beneath a lamp. Diego glanced at me, his brow lifting in a question. I answered with a subtle nod.

We settled together, the night air brushing gently against my skin as he draped one arm around me. The way his gaze lingered on me sent a tingling warmth straight through my stomach, once again awakening feelings I thought I had left behind long ago.

The noise from the club had already faded into a distant blur, replaced by the softer sounds of the city around us. Lights shimmered above in neon colors, yet this bench felt like a space carved just for us.

Diego shifted, turning slightly so his focus remained entirely on me. His hand lifted until his palm cupped my cheek. The warmth of his touch drew me closer effortlessly. My body wanted to shudder at the intensity of it, yet I resisted, instead leaning the slightest bit nearer until the distance between us nearly vanished.

"I can't get you out of my head," he murmured, his lips so close that the words seemed to vibrate against my skin. "I know it's only been a single day, but being with you feels like something I haven't known in years, and I want to see where it takes us, if you'll let me."

"Diego," I whispered , and before I could form another word, he closed the distance between us, his lips pressing firmly against mine. In that instant, the world seemed to vanish completely. Every sound faded, and every thought dissolved, until all that remained was the sensation of his mouth on mine. Tingling warmth spread through my body like wildfire, kept nerves I had forgotten existed. A muffled breath escaped against his lips as I trembled in his arms, overwhelmed by the simple truth that I wanted nothing more than to draw him closer.

The kiss stretched endlessly, carrying us further away from the noise of everything else. Neither of us broke away until the lack of air forced us into small, uneven breaths. My hands moved instinctively, brushing against his shoulders, his arms, his back, while his fingers touched me in return. The wandering was restrained, though, lingering only in places that felt respectful, yet the intensity was undeniable. I released another shaky breath when he finally pulled away, his eyes searching mine.

"I meant it when I said it," he whispered, resting his forehead against mine. "I've never felt this way before."

I hesitated, caught between the urge to speak and the inability to find words that could capture the chaos inside me. It had been years since I had felt chemistry like this with anyone. A part of me wanted to be cautious and hold back to protect myself and keep the moment light and fleeting. Another part of me could not deny the pull between us— into two sentences , and every word between us felt natural, as though it had always been meant to happen. People often advised taking things slowly and guarding your heart, yet with Diego, none of that mattered.

"Neither have I," I admitted softly at last, my chest tightening as my heart pounded against my ribs. This connection might remain nothing more than a memory, tucked into what could easily become one of the most unforgettable weekends of my life.

Still, a quiet voice inside me refused to let go of the truth. If I wanted things to go further than that, there was a part of my life I had not revealed to him yet—might change everything.

"With that said,, there is something I need to tell you …" My voice trembled slightly as I searched his expression. For a moment, I caught the way his features tightened as though he was bracing for the worst. Not wanting to leave that tension lingering, I quickly pushed forward before he had the chance to imagine scenarios far worse than the truth.

"There is a reason why I am so tied to Houston, and it's not only because of my work. I am a single mother to a six-year-old girl, and she is my entire world. I know that may be a lot to take in, so I will understand if you need time to …"

I never finished my sentence. Diego shook his head firmly, cutting off the thought before it could gain ground. "Is that all?"

His words caught me off guard. My brow arched in surprise as I tried to process what he had just asked. Slowly, almost uncertainly, I nodded. "Yes, that is all. Though it would change everything for many people, you know." Even as I said it, the way he looked at me told me that, for him, nothing would change.

"Not for me," he murmured. His eyes locked with mine, filled with a heat that nearly stole my breath. It was clear from the way he leaned toward me that resisting another kiss was taking all the strength he had. "That does not change anything for me. I still feel the same way about you. I still want you just as much as I did a minute ago."

Those words struck something inside me that had been hidden for longer than I cared to admit. A part of me I thought I had buried suddenly stirred, awakening with undeniable force. Desire, raw and consuming, burned through me—desire to be touched, to be held, to surrender to the moment without fear.

How reckless would it be to give in to that?

Yet with Diego's arm still around me, it didn't feel reckless at all. And so, for the first time in my life, I made the first move.

"Then why don't you show me that?" I whispered, leaning close until my lips brushed against his. My voice faltered slightly, though my intent was clear. "Maybe you can take me to your hotel room."

Surprise flickered in his eyes, though it quickly softened into something else, desire. He nodded slowly, his hands reaching for mine as his fingers laced with my own. Without hesitation, he rose from the bench, guiding me with him. Step by step, we left the bench behind and began walking back toward the hotel. Luckily, it wasn't far, which only made the anticipation grow stronger with each moment.

We barely reached the elevator before his hands found me once more, and his lips collided against mine once again. A small, muffled moan escaped me as my back pressed against the cool mirror behind me, my body pinned against him in a way that told me he wanted every part of me.

"I want you so badly," he whispered against my lips, his breath hot and uneven. "You have no idea. I don't even understand how someone I have only known for hours can make me feel this way …" His voice came out rough, each word brushing over my skin as his mouth moved against mine. My fingers clutched at the collar of his shirt, tugging him closer. His hand slid higher along my thigh, sparking a shiver that travelled up my spine, leaving me trembling with need.

The elevator door opened suddenly with a loud *ding*, breaking through the heat of the moment. Relief washed over me when I realized no one was standing on the other side to witness what we were doing. For a brief second, we both stood still, our breathing ragged, our eyes locked in unspoken agreement that nothing could pull us apart now.

Diego wasted no time before intertwining his fingers with mine, tugging me gently yet firmly out of the elevator and down the long hallway. My pulse raced with each step. When we reached his room, he swiped the key through the lock, and the door clicked open. I barely managed to glance at the space before he pulled me back into his arms, our mouths met once more for a kiss that left me breathless.

"I have never felt this before," he said again, as if it were some holy mantra he couldn't stop repeating, his lips brushing over mine as he spoke. A small voice in the back of my mind reminded me that many men probably spoke like this, yet with him, I believed every single word. Perhaps it was reckless, yet the conviction in his eyes and the fire in his touch left no room for doubt.

Desire rose through me with a force that bordered on unbearable, filling every part of me with a hunger that demanded to be satisfied. My chest rose and fell in uneven breaths as I pressed closer, desperate to feel his body against mine. My lips clung to his, refusing to let go, while tingles of anticipation rippled through me with every soft graze of his fingers on my skin.

A soft moan slipped from my lips, and the sound seemed to stir something raw inside him that matched the hunger already burning within me. His hands lingered at my hips as I remained pressed against the wall, yet his gaze softened , softening as he looked directly into my eyes.

"Are you sure you want this? If you're not—"

"I want this," I cut him off gently, cupping his face with both hands and drawing him closer until our foreheads nearly touched. I could not remember the last time I wanted anything as much as I wanted this right now.

Those words were enough. His lips claimed mine once more, only this time the kiss burned hotter and hungrier, as if he could no longer hold himself back. His arms wrapped around me, lifting me effortlessly, and within a few swift strides, he carried me to the bed. The world tilted slightly before he laid me down on the cool sheets, his body pressing over mine.

My pulse thundered as his hands travelled along my sides, fingers curling into the fabric of my dress until he began tugging it upward, freeing me from its hold. My own hands moved just as urgently, sliding over his chest before gripping the edge of his shirt. I pulled it over his head in one quick motion, revealing skin that made my breath catch. My fingers found the waistband of his shorts next, pushing them down until the last barriers between us were almost gone.

The sight of him stole the air from my lungs. His body looked like it had been carved by ancient gods, with perfect muscles and flawless skin. Heat rushed through me as I took in the reality of him so close while I lay beneath him with only the thin barrier of my underwear left.

"You're so damn beautiful …" he murmured, his gaze sweeping over every part of me with hunger that made me shiver.

"Diego …" I moaned softly before he took only a moment to yank his underwear down, freeing himself. He reached into his nightstand, grabbing a small package that he quickly tore open before rolling the protection down over his shaft, that was already hard and ready for me. In a heartbeat, he was on top of me again, with his length pressing against my crotch, and nothing but the thin lace of my underwear separating us.

"Please," I pleaded, unable to handle a single moment more of this torture.

His fingers swept down my body, caressing me inch by inch, until he found the edge of my panties, pushing them to the side for easier access Another small moan left my lips as he leaned down, pressing his mouth to my throat.

"You're so wet …" he murmured, his fingers sweeping across my pussy. A small whimper escaped my lips against my will, and my eyes closed as I tilted my head back. His fingertips moved over all the right places, sending tingles through my body that I couldn't control, until he positioned himself at my entrance and slowly, oh so slowly, pushed himself inside me.

A slight pang of pain spread through me, mixing with pleasure unlike any other. A small, soundless gasp escaped my lips as my eyes rolled back, my back arching beneath him in response to the wave of sensation that rumbled through me.

"Fuck …" he groaned into my neck, moving his hips back and forth while maintaining that slow pace. Each time he slide back in, though, he'd allow his cock to move inside me just a little further, making my whole-body tremble.

"Diego …" I panted once more, one of my hands tangling into his hair, while the other dragged down his strong back, nails sinking into his skin. He slid deeper into me, reaching all the right corners inside me. I throbbed around his thickness, soaking him in my arousal, as I wrapped my legs around him, only to pull him in closer.

That was the only thing he needed to consume me entirely.

In one deeper thrust, he filled me up more, now setting a steadier pace. My eyes fluttered open, though I could barely focus on my surroundings as pleasure pumped through me. His lips were all over me—my chin and jaw, my throat, my chest. Diego trailed hungry kisses everywhere he could reach, until I was trembling from the sensation that consumed me whole.

"You feel so good, and you're so fucking beautiful when you take me like this," he swore under his breath, and the filthiness of his words only aroused me more … until I could no longer take it and began lifting my hips toward him, too.

One of his hands clutched my hip, while the other found its way between my thighs, settling on my clit and rubbing it in a slow, circular motion, an odd contrast to the way he rammed himself into me. Each thrust brought more pleasure , like a current about to sweep me away whole, and I had no choice but to surrender to it.

My lips parted, moans tearing free from my throat as my body began trembling, as if it no longer belonged to me at all. I gasped for air as Diego raised me to those blissful heights where my body threatened to shatter under pressure at any moment

"That's it," he murmured breathlessly, his body tense on top of mine, "that's my good girl. I want to see you come for me. I want to see the pleasure on your face and hear the sounds you make ..."

Something about those words was my undoing. Two more thrusts were all it took before pleasure struck me—hard, and a loud moan escaped my lips, echoing through the room. My orgasm spread through me mercilessly, from the base of my spine, all the way to my limbs, until I was a shaking, quivering mess beneath him, barely able to breathe.

"Diego, I—"

"I got you, baby," he whispered against my ear as I continued to shudder, still affected by my first orgasm, but he didn't seem to be done. I had never experienced something like it—despite being so tender from having just come, I could feel another one building with the way he thrust into me and the sound of his moans echoing in my ears. I gripped his shoulders, holding onto him tightly, until I felt him tense on top of me and release a loud grunt that lingered at the back of his throat as he came. Right then, that bliss spread through me once more, darkening my vision and making it difficult to breathe. And I enjoyed every single second of it.

Afterward, we lay tangled in each other's arms, the world outside the hotel room forgotten. Diego brushed a kiss against my forehead, his touch gentle and reassuring. "I'm so glad you're here," he murmured, his voice filled with tenderness.

I smiled, a contented sigh escaping my lips. "Me too," I replied softly.

Diego pulled me closer, his fingers tracing patterns on my skin. "When this trip ends, I want to see you again," he said earnestly. "Would you consider visiting me in Miami? Or maybe I could come to Houston?"

I hesitated for a moment, the reality of our separate lives looming over us once more. "Diego, I have Sophie," I reminded him gently, a pang of guilt tugging at my heart.

He nodded understandingly, brushing a kiss against my shoulder. "I know. Take your time. When you're ready, I'll be here."

I closed my eyes, letting the warmth of his hands anchor me as our connection stretched across the space between us, fragile yet undeniable. It stung to know the future was uncertain. For now, I chose to focus on the present, the heat of his gaze, the way his fingers intertwined with mine, and the soft rhythm of his breathing next to mine.

As the night wore on, neither of us could sleep, and our conversation softened into whispers, words laden with shared secrets and quiet confessions.

"I used to wear mismatched shoes to school," I admitted with a grin. "And I didn't notice until halfway through the day. I thought I was so stylish."

Diego laughed, a warm, low sound that made my chest flutter. "Stylish, huh? Bold choice. I admire the confidence."

"Confidence? More like obliviousness," I said, nudging him playfully. "But hey, fashion is subjective."

He shook his head, still chuckling. "You've got style in all the right ways, though I can't say I've ever had mismatched shoes on the field."

I raised an eyebrow. "Oh, did you have your own fashion disasters?"

He groaned dramatically. "My first big game didn't exactly go as planned. I tripped over my own feet and fell face-first in front of the crowd. Everyone clapped. I think it was pity claps."

I laughed, leaning closer. "That's tragic. Were you okay?"

"I survived," he said, smirking. "And I learned two things: always tie my cleats tight and never underestimate the power of a good crowd reaction."

I nudged him again, laughing softly. "Well, I'd pay to see that. Maybe one day you can recreate it for me?"

He caught my hand, brushing his thumb over my knuckles, and leaned in slightly. "If you insist. But I have a feeling your stories are going to be harder to beat."

"Challenge accepted," I whispered, feeling my stomach flutter as our laughter faded into a comfortable quiet.

When the first light of dawn spilled over the glittering Vegas skyline, I rested my head against his chest, feeling the steady beat of his heart beneath my ear. At that quiet moment, I realized something terrifying and straightforward all at once—no matter where life would take us, Diego had already carved a place in my story, one I wasn't sure I could ever let go of.

Seven
Amelia

The sunlight spilled through the hotel curtains, painting gold stripes across the bed. Diego was still asleep; one arm draped over the pillow the other stretched toward my side. I watched him for a moment, taking in the way he relaxed so completely, something I rarely got to see in anyone.

"You're awake," he murmured, his voice rough and lazy.

"I am," I said, stretching. "Only because someone is hogging the blankets."

He cracked one eye open, smirking. "Terrible liar."

I rolled my eyes but smiled. "You're too confident for someone who drools in his sleep."

"I do not drool," he said, turning onto his side. "You just don't want to admit you like waking up next to me."

For a moment, I stayed quiet, letting the tug in my chest pass without comment. It wasn't love, not even infatuation. It was just something unexpected.

Diego pushed himself up on an elbow. "One more day," he said. "Let's make it count. Fremont Street, photo booth, whatever feels fun."

I laughed softly. "You really are determined to make this weekend unforgettable, huh?"

"Mission accomplished?" he teased.

"Maybe," I admitted, already feeling the pull of excitement. I quickly texted Victoria and Anastasia to see if this would be fine, and got a response in less than a second telling me to 'go for it.'

By mid-morning, we were out the door, sneakers pounding against the pavement as the energy of Fremont Street wrapped around us. Diego ran ahead, tossing playful challenges over his shoulder, and I chased after him, laughing when he pretended not to hear me. Street performers, neon lights, and the scent of popcorn and roasted nuts filled the air, making everything feel dizzyingly alive.

Eventually, we ducked into a tiny photobooth tucked into the corner of a casino arcade. We crammed together into the small space, and Diego immediately made a ridiculous face, earning a laugh from me.

"You're cheating," I teased.

"Cheating at what?" he asked, grinning.

"Being the cutest person in the world," I grumbled, rolling my eyes even as I smiled.

He leaned closer, his face just inches from mine, and for a second, the world outside the booth disappeared. "My God, you're so beautiful," he murmured, eyes locked on mine.

Heat rose to my cheeks, and then there was a flutter in my stomach that made me forget to tease back. Before I could speak, he brushed his lips to mine, gentle and warm. The camera flashed just as our lips met, capturing a perfect, fleeting moment of connection.

When we pulled apart, we laughed softly, hearts racing in sync. I leaned my head against his shoulder for the next few shots, letting him make silly faces while I tried, and failed, to look composed. The camera clicked again and again, but I barely noticed.

Later, we wandered through street vendors, shared bites of candy, and dared each other to try ridiculous games. Diego's competitiveness made me laugh, and I realized I was noticing things I hadn't before, the way his eyes lit up when he won, the way he made room for me to tease him back, and the quiet attentiveness that made me feel seen even in a crowd.

As the sun dipped lower, we found a quiet rooftop overlooking the Strip. I leaned back, taking in the glowing city below. Diego handed me a soda and nudged me gently.

"This," he said, his voice soft, "might be my favorite part of the weekend."

"Hmm." I smiled faintly. "It's hard to choose, but this view. It's pretty close."

He tilted his head, his eyes soft. "You know, I could get used to moments like this."

"Careful," I said, smirking. "You might make me start imagining things."

"Good," he said, grinning. "That's exactly the point."

Finally, I glanced at my phone. The girls were probably wondering where I'd disappeared to. "I should check on them," I said reluctantly, brushing a strand of hair from my face.

Diego nodded, that sly grin returning. "Brunch tomorrow," he said, voice low and promising. "Everyone together. My treat. You in?"

I smirked. "I'll be there. But only because I expect you to pay for my coffee."

"Deal," he said, eyes twinkling. "And don't think you're getting out of more photobooth pictures before the end of the weekend."

I laughed, shaking my head. "We'll see about that."

I waved and headed back toward the girls, my heart lighter than it had been in months. The day with Diego had been everything I didn't know I needed: playful, exciting, and easy.

The weekend had been a blur of laughter, champagne, and too little sleep. Between brunches, late-night dinners, and those impulsive Vegas moments that seemed to stretch forever, Diego and I had slipped into an easy rhythm that felt both new and familiar. Victoria was wrapped up in Taije, Anastasia had found her own distraction, and for once, I let myself exist without overthinking.

But now, as I zipped up my suitcase, reality grounded me again. Vegas magic only lasted so long before real life came calling.

My phone buzzed.

Victoria:

Are you ready? Last brunch before we head out.

Me:

On my way. See you soon.

I gave the room a final glance, then slung my bag over my shoulder and headed down. The air in the lobby buzzed with goodbyes—the kind that only happen after a weekend you didn't expect to mean something.

At the restaurant, Diego's face lit up the second he saw me.

"Hey, Amelia," he said, pulling out my chair. His voice was warm, familiar now in a way that made something in me soften.

"Hey," I returned, offering a small smile as I sat down. Brunch flowed easily with conversations about our time in Vegas. Diego and I traded looks across the table, small smiles that said more than either of us admitted out loud.

"So," he said, his tone light but his eyes searching mine, "I have to ask again. What do you think about the summer? I could come to Houston, or maybe you can visit Miami."

I hesitated. Not because I did not want to, but because it sounded dangerously close to *real.* "You don't waste time, do you?" I teased, trying to keep it playful.

He grinned. "When I know what I want, I go for it."

"Hmm," I said, smirking as I lifted my coffee cup. "And what is it you think you want?"

His gaze lingered. "You."

For a second, I didn't say anything. I just looked at him, and tried to figure out what this weekend had done to me. I was not the kind of woman who fell fast or easy. But Diego had this energy, this quiet confidence that drew me in despite every wall I'd built.

"Diego," I started, choosing my words carefully. "You've been … unexpected. In a good way. But my life isn't simple. I have Sophie, and Houston, and—"

He nodded before I could finish. "I know this won't be simple."

That earned a small laugh from me. "Good, because I don't do simple, apparently."

His hand brushed mine under the table, just briefly. "Then don't overthink it. Just … don't forget about this."

"I won't," I said quietly, and meant it.

When brunch ended, the group lingered outside the restaurant, reluctant to let the weekend go. The sun was sharp, the Vegas heat pressing down on us as we made our way to the rideshare pickup area. Taije helped the girls with their luggage, and Diego fell in step beside me, his hand brushing mine once as we walked.

The air between us was quieter now, a mix of exhaustion and something unspoken. The city buzzed around us, but it felt like we were in our own small pocket of stillness.

"Guess this is it," he said when we reached the curb.

"Yeah," I exhaled, trying to sound casual. "Back to real life."

Diego smiled, that soft, teasing grin that had somehow worked its way under my skin. "I could get used to this version of real life a little longer."

I rolled my eyes lightly, though my lips curved. "You say that now. You haven't seen me juggling early meetings and school drop-offs."

He chuckled. "I'd still take it."

Before I could respond, my phone buzzed, notifying me that the driver was pulling up. I turned toward the approaching car, trying to ignore the slight, sharp tug in my chest. Diego reached into his jacket pocket, hesitating for half a second before holding something out to me: a small strip of photobooth pictures from the day before. Our laughter frozen in frames, that kiss we shared, and his hand on my jaw.

"Souvenir," he said, his eyes tracing my face. "Because if I could freeze time, it would be that moment … you laughing like that beside me."

I felt my throat tighten as I took them. "Like I could ever forget that."

I looked at him then, noticing the sun catching the edge of his jaw. "Careful," I said softly. "I might actually take you up on that."

He grinned, slow and sure. "I hope you do."

The driver opened the trunk, and I slid my bag inside. Diego leaned in and kissed me. It was unhurried sure, the kind of kiss that promised more without asking for it.

When I pulled away, I felt lighter somehow. Not in love, not heartbroken … just awake.

I got in quickly. I couldn't bear to look back at him. As the car door shut and the city blurred past the window, I caught my reflection: sun-warmed skin, and eyes bright in a way they hadn't been in a long time.

Vegas might have been fleeting, but what it stirred in me wasn't.

Eight
Diego

The celebration in Vegas had been wild. Champagne. Music. A blur of flashing lights and noise. Winning the championship should have been the highlight of it all, but now, sitting by the pool back in Miami, the memory that refused to fade wasn't the trophy. It was her.

Amelia.

There was something about her that had burrowed under my skin, something I couldn't shake. I had met plenty of women, beautiful, confident, and charming, but Amelia was different. She carried herself like she had somewhere to be, someone to love, and did not need anyone to complete the picture.

And maybe that was what got me.

I leaned back in the lounge chair, the Florida sun sharp against my skin, and tried to focus on the sound of the water. It did not help.

Taije dropped into the chair next to me, sunglasses on, drink in hand. "You have been staring at nothing for ten minutes, bro. You good?"

"Yeah," I said, though it came out flat.

He chuckled. "Let me guess. Amelia?"

I exhaled through my nose, shaking my head. "You make it sound like I have got it bad."

"Do you?"

I didn't answer right away. "I do not know. It's just … she is different. She was not chasing the spotlight, and she did not care about who I was or what I did. It was just easy."

Taije grinned. "Easy? That is not what I remember about Vegas. Nothing about that weekend was easy, man."

I smirked despite myself. "You know what I mean."

He turned his head toward me. "You ever think maybe that is why she has got you twisted up? She is not like the girls we meet on the road. She is not looking for a post-game story."

"Yeah," I said quietly. "She's got her own story."

The thought hung there between us.

I remembered the way Amelia had talked about her daughter. The way her eyes softened when she mentioned her. I was not used to that kind of love. My world was built around structure: training, travel, and stadium lights. Everything in it revolved around performance. Amelia's revolved around something real, and it scared the hell out of me. Yet at the same time, it captured my curiosity like nothing had in a long time.

Taije broke the silence. "You thinking of seeing her again?"

"Eventually," I said, dragging a hand through my hair. "I mean, I would like to, but she's in Houston, I'm here. Season is starting soon. I do not even know where she stands on all this."

"She probably thinks you are just another guy she met in Vegas," he said.

"Maybe." I looked out over the water, the sunlight shimmering on the surface. "But it did not feel like that. Not for me."

He studied me for a moment, then grinned. "You, my friend, are in trouble."

I laughed, shaking my head. "It is not that deep."

"Uh-huh." He leaned back, smirking. "Keep telling yourself that."

I went quiet after that, letting the conversation fade. But even as we sat there, surrounded by noise and laughter, I couldn't stop replaying moments in my head, her laugh echoing off the photo booth

walls, the look in her eyes before she walked away, and that kiss goodbye that still lingered on my lips.

That night, the city felt louder than usual, Miami heat clinging to the air, car horns echoing somewhere down the boulevard. I had the game highlights playing on TV, volume low, a beer sweating on the table beside me.

I should have felt proud. We had made history. My phone kept lighting up with messages, agents, teammates, fans, but none of it hit the same. Every time the screen went dark, I caught myself waiting for it to light up again, but with her name on it.

Taije's voice replayed in my head. *You are in trouble.*

Maybe he was right.

I scrolled through the photos from Vegas, half smiling at the chaos, crowded clubs, champagne sprays, blurred lights.

And then there it was, a single picture from Fremont Street. Amelia and I in the photobooth. Her head tilted toward me, my hand on her jaw. The shot was off-center, half our faces cut off, but her smile, God, *it looked real.*

I leaned back, phone still in hand.

She was a mom. She had a life, one that didn't revolve around football schedules and away games. And I respected that more than I wanted to admit.

I thought about the way she laughed when she beat me at the ring toss, how she rolled her eyes when I called her beautiful, how she had walked away at the airport without looking back. That last part stuck with me the most.

For the first time in a long while, I was not thinking about the next match or the next win. I was thinking about a woman in Houston who probably had no idea how much she had gotten under my skin.

The phone buzzed once on the table. Not her, just a team update. *Figures.*

I drained the rest of my beer and stood, heading out onto the balcony. The city lights stretched endlessly, humming with life. Somewhere beneath all that noise, I felt a shift, slight, inconvenient, but real.

Nine
Amelia

As I stepped into the arrivals area, people moved around me, each of them lost in the webs of their own lives … and then I found mine. My heart lifted at the sight of Sophie's beaming face. My mother and Sophie stood by the railing, waving as soon as they spotted me.

Sophie broke into a sprint, her little arms stretched wide. I dropped my bag and bent down just in time to catch her.

"Mommy, I missed you so much!" she squealed, burying her face against my neck.

"I missed you, too, sweet girl," I said, kissing the top of her head. Her hair smelled faintly of strawberries and bubble-gum shampoo. "Did you have fun with Nana and Papa?"

She nodded so hard her curls bounced. "Mommy, guess what! We made pancakes *and* cookies, and I helped Nana fold the towels—but I messed up the corners —but I messed up the corners."

I laughed, brushing her cheek. "That sounds like a very important job."

"And we went to the park! Papa pushed me so high on the swings that I almost touched the sky. And I drew you a picture—it's in the car!"

"You did? I can't wait to see it."

Sophie continued, her words spilling out faster than I could keep up. She spun around in her pink dress, trying to let all her thoughts come out—at once. "Oh, and Papa let me stay up late to watch a movie, and we had popcorn, and—Mommy—there was this cat outside the porch that looked just like the one in the movie! I think it wanted to come inside!"

I smiled, my heart softening with every excited breath she took. Her world was so full, so simple, and so beautifully hers.

As we walked toward baggage claim, she slipped her small hand into mine and looked up at me. "Did you have fun on your trip?"

"I did," I said honestly. "It was nice to get away for a little while."

Sophie nodded thoughtfully, as if that made perfect sense. "I'm glad you're home now. Everything's more fun when you're here."

Her words hit somewhere deep. Listening to her chatter, the noise and exhaustion of travel melted away. This was my life, the one I built, the one that mattered most.

And at that moment, I felt grounded again.

Later, as I unpacked, my phone buzzed. I looked down and saw a message from Diego flash across my screen. My heart dropped instantly as I read it.

Diego:

Hey Amelia, did you make it back to
Houston safely?

A smile tugged at my lips despite myself. I quickly replied.

Me:

Yes, just got home. It's good to be back. How was
your flight back to Miami?

Diego:

It was smooth. Glad to hear you're
safe back home. I still hope we can see
each other again soon. Please think
about my offer.

I felt a flutter in my chest at his words. Our connection was undeniable, and the thought of spending more time with him was tempting. But I hesitated, thinking of all the reasons why this could be a mistake. Diego was a handsome soccer player with a demanding schedule and unlimited options. What did he want with a single mother like me? What if it didn't work out, and he hurt me? I was overthinking, talking myself out of taking a chance on starting anything new with anyone, but that wasn't anything new. Ever since Brad, I had sworn that I'd never let myself get hurt like that again. And Diego's message remained unanswered.

The next morning at Elite Source, my mind kept wandering back to the weekend. I sat at my desk, trying to focus on the latest marketing campaign, but Diego's face kept intruding on my thoughts. The chemistry we'd shared was undeniable, and the way he had talked about spending the summer together had planted a seed of possibility that I couldn't ignore. But could I really consider spending time with Diego this summer? A long-distance romance seemed so impractical, especially at this age.

He lived in Miami, and I was rooted in Houston with Sophie. The logistics alone were daunting. Yet, the memories of our passionate time together in Vegas were still fresh in my mind, and the idea of seeing him again, away from the pressures of work and everyday life, was tempting.

Just as I was beginning to lose myself in thoughts of Diego's smile once again, Lisa interrupted me. "Amelia, Mr. Thompson is asking for the latest analytics for our May campaign. He needs them ASAP."

I nodded, shaking off the daydreams momentarily. "Okay, I'll get on that right away. Thanks, Lisa."

Turning my attention back to my computer screen, I pulled up the necessary data and started compiling the analytics report.

Numbers and graphs filled my screen, but Diego's face kept popping into my mind, distracting me from the task at hand. But more than his face, it was the memories of our passionate moment together in bed that flooded my brain. I found myself blushing at the thought, trying to shake off the distraction.

Just then, Mr. Thompson walked past my desk. "Any progress on those analytics for Dolce?" Dolce was an ice cream chain and one of our smaller clients, but still important, nonetheless. Each of my clients got my full attention and dedication, and they were no exception.

"I'm working on it right now, Mr. Thompson," I assured him.

He nodded and moved on to check in with another team member. I refocused on the report, pushing thoughts of Diego and our shared moments to the back of my mind. This was my job and my career, and I needed to give it my full attention.

As I wrapped up the day at work, I glanced at the clock. It was time to leave and pick up Sophie. Just as I gathered my things and headed towards the door, my phone buzzed again. The familiar chime of the Three Musketeers group chat caught my attention.

I quickly unlocked my phone to find a flurry of messages from Victoria and Anastasia, as I expected.

Victoria:

Amelia, have you talked to Diego since you got back?

Anastasia:

Yeah, girl! Spill the tea! What's the latest?

I hesitated, then typed a response.

Me:

He reached out. He wants to see me again. But I don't know, I guess I'm just second-guessing myself, you guys. He's a soccer player, and there are probably so many women throwing themselves at him. Why would he choose a girl like me and a single mom at that?

Victoria:

Because you're incredible, that's why. You're strong, accomplished, smart, and absolutely beautiful. Don't sell yourself short, Mel..

Anastasia:

Exactly! You've been through so much, and you deserve to be happy. Don't let your fears hold you back. Take a chance on happiness.

Me:

But what about Sophie? What if it doesn't work out?

Victoria:

Sophie adores you, and she'll want to see you happy. We'll help you figure it out. Even if I have to babysit, we've got your back! Give Diego a chance to show you what he's made of.

Anastasia:

Let him spoil you a little. You deserve it, girl.

Starting the engine, I drove out of the parking lot, the warmth of the Texas sun filling the car. The idea of seeing Diego again, of exploring what could be, brought a mix of nervousness and excitement, but I still hesitated. I had burned myself once, and I didn't want it to happen to me again.

As I drove towards Sophie's school, though, the group chat buzzed with messages of encouragement and excitement. Their support sparked a newfound confidence in me, and when I pulled up in front of Sophie's school, I decided to take action. This could be something good for me, but I wouldn't know unless I tried.

I grabbed my phone, hesitating for a moment before typing a message that could change everything.

Me:

How about we give it a chance, Diego? Your city or mine?

Ten

Amelia

Miami loosened something in me the second the airport doors slid open and the heat wrapped around my skin—salt, jet fuel, and the faintest whisper of ocean. I followed the current of arriving passengers, heart thudding in a rhythm I already knew. Him.

I spotted Diego before he saw me—cap low, gray tee, and an easy posture that made him look like he belonged everywhere and nowhere all at once. Then his gaze lifted, and when he found me, his mouth curved into that familiar smile that made the world tilt a little.

I ran straight to him. He caught me easily, his arms strong around my waist. For a heartbeat, the noise of the airport disappeared. His lips brushed mine, soft and steady, and I forgot about everything except how right it felt to finally be here.

"It's really you," he murmured against my cheek.

"I told you I was coming," I said, though my voice came out quieter than I meant.

"Yeah." He smiled. "But wanting something and getting it aren't always the same."

He took my bag and laced his fingers through mine as we moved toward the exit. I almost pulled my hand back—an instinct I had learned somewhere along the way—but then his thumb brushed the inside of my wrist, slow and gentle, and I let it stay.

Outside, the Miami heat pressed close. He opened the car door for me, that old-school gesture I had forgotten I missed.

"Still a gentleman," I teased.

"Selective," he said. "Only for you."

As he drove, the city opened up—palms, sunlight, a wash of color that made everything feel alive. His right hand rested on the console, fingers brushing mine again, testing.

"How was the flight?" he asked.

"Uneventful," I said. "The woman next to me watched three true-crime shows in a row, so … I was entertained for the most part."

He laughed, eyes crinkling at the corners. "You could've texted. I would've sent you a playlist."

"I didn't want to bother you." The words slipped out before I could stop them.

Diego looked at me. "You could never bother me." Something in the way he said it made me look out the window. I wasn't used to people saying things like that and meaning them.

We fell into easy conversation, the kind that lived somewhere between comfort and curiosity. He told me stories about Miami and about running near the inlet in the mornings when it was still quiet.

"Do you think about soccer when you run?" I nudged him playfully.

"Sometimes," he said, "sometimes I think about nothing. And sometimes I think about you."

I smiled, and my heart did that small, ridiculous stutter. "That's a lot of pressure for an early morning."

He glanced over. "It's motivation."

The closer we got to his apartment, the more real everything became. Part of me wanted to turn back, to stay in the safety of wanting instead of having—but I had promised myself I would stop running from the good things.

When we arrived at Diego's condo, I was taken aback by its elegance. The building itself was a modern marvel of glass and steel, rising above the city. Diego led me through the sleek lobby and up to his condo. As the door swung open, I was greeted by an expanse of polished marble floors, floor-to-ceiling windows, and breathtaking views of the ocean.

"Wow, this place is incredible, "I said, my voice filled with awe as I took in the luxurious surroundings.

Diego smiled, wrapping his arms around me from behind. "I'm glad you like it. I want you to feel comfortable here."

And for a moment, I did.

The living room was tastefully decorated with modern furniture, a large sectional couch, and abstract art adorning the walls. The kitchen was a chef's dream, with stainless steel appliances and a massive island that looked perfect for casual breakfast or late-night conversations.

"This is so different from my place," I admitted, feeling a twinge of self-consciousness as I thought of my cozy, slightly cluttered apartment.

Diego chuckled, pressing a kiss to my forehead. "I have an idea to help you settle in. How about a date night? I know a great restaurant by the beach. We can have dinner, walk along the shore, and enjoy each other's company."

My heart fluttered at the thought. "That sounds perfect."

"Great," Diego said, his eyes lighting up with excitement. "I'll make the reservation, and we can head out in a bit. But first, let me give you the grand tour of the rest of my place."

The restaurant was a charming seaside eatery with fairy lights strung. The air smelled like salt and citrus, and when he poured the wine, I couldn't help but think of how easy this all felt. Too easy, maybe.

"Tell me about your off-season," I asked. I wanted to know everything there was to know about him.

He leaned back, relaxed. "It's been relaxing and fun, now that I have time to focus on the important things in life. Things that are real and what matter most."

"Real," I repeated. "That's hard to find."

He smiled faintly. "Sometimes you stop looking when you've already found it."

The words sat between us, quiet and steady. I looked down at my glass, afraid he might see too much if I didn't. We talked for hours—about Sophie, about Houston, and about the long way he'd come from Argentina. By the time the plates were cleared, the sun had melted into gold behind the water, yet there was still so much I wanted to talk say.

"Come on," he said, standing. "Let's walk."

We left our shoes by the railing and wandered down the sand, the tide chasing our feet. The city lights flickered behind us, soft and distant.

"I was scared to come here," I admitted, my voice low.

He glanced over. "Scared of me?"

"Scared of what it might mean. What if this—us—was just a moment? What if I ruined it by trying to make it real?" I shook my head. Thoughts raced through my mind, but in his presence, they all became just a little quieter.

He reached for my hand. "And now?"

He smiled, brushing his thumb over my knuckles. "Now, I think it's the good kind of scared."

Back at his apartment, the silence hummed around us. We'd barely managed to keep our hands off each other as we made it back. His fingers trailed mine as if asking permission. I gave it without words.

"I want you," he murmured, showering my neck with soft kisses that had goosebumps roll down my skin. It was a struggle not to shudder against him, to keep some sense of composure so I didn't feel as exposed. Even if, for once, I didn't mind letting my guard down.

"Then take me," I whispered in return. He didn't need any further encouragement. His hands were on me, slowly removing the dress I wore. Black silk slipped down my body, and the worship I caught in his gaze aroused me beyond any comprehension. My lips parted as his kisses drifted lower, and I bit my bottom lip, watching the way his hands moved across my body , slow and deliberate as if he was memorizing every curve.

"You're so beautiful," he whispered, and something about those words was my undoing. I needed him so much closer.

"Diego, please ..." I whimpered, the arousal pounding inside me. He didn't waste another moment; slowly, he removed his shirt, revealing the muscular physique beneath, and then his pants followed. As always, he rolled the protection on his shaft before he was on top of me, kissing me everywhere as he prodded against my entrance.

My eyes rolled back into my skull as I finally felt him slide deep inside me. With how aroused I was, the motion was almost frictionless, and I found myself arching my back in sheer pleasure. My nails dug into his skin, as if that would somehow help me anchor myself through the pleasure.

"I can feel how much you enjoy this," he murmured against my ear, his tone low and blending with his heavy breaths. It drove me inward, to the point where I felt like I was losing myself. "I can feel you throb ..."

In a heartbeat, I placed my hands on his shoulders and spun us around. Diego got the idea of what I wanted to do; I wanted to be on the top and control the motion. His eyes were locked on mine as I rested my hands against his chest, moving my hips in a slow, circular motion.

Pleasure flooded me; he was reaching spots inside me that I didn't even know existed, and had my entire body tremble. It was a sensation unlike any other, making it difficult to think clearly.

"Just like that ..." he grunted, "show me how much you want me, baby."

And I wanted him. My God, how I wanted him. I wanted this love to devour us both.

His words prompted me to move quicker. Harder. I chased that pleasure with his hands on my hips and his gaze on me, until I could no longer handle it. I leaned down, hungrily kissing him. As our lips collided, more pleasure tingled through me, and before I knew it, my orgasm rumbled through me, hard and merciless. A loud moan broke from my lips as I arched my back, whimpering against his mouth as I trembled, until I felt him grip my hips tighter, tensing underneath me as his pleasure struck, too. Neither of us could move for a long moment, and it still felt just right.

Later, lying beside him, I traced a line along his arm and whispered, "You feel like home."

His reply came against my skin. "Then don't let go." And I didn't.

The next morning, sunlight slipped through the curtains, warm and golden. I woke to the sound of clinking dishes and the faint scent of coffee drifting from the kitchen. For a moment, I lay there, letting myself sink into the quiet hum of his apartment—the ocean outside, the distant buzz of the city, and the space beside me still warm from where Diego had been.

When I padded out, he was standing at the counter, shirtless, a towel draped over his shoulder, flipping something in a pan.

"You cook?" I asked, my voice still rough with sleep.

He turned, flashing that boyish grin. "Only when I'm trying to impress someone."

"Then I'm definitely impressed," I said, sliding onto one of the barstools.

He set a plate in front of me—eggs, fruit, and toast. It was simple, but thoughtful.

"Breakfast à la Alvarez," he announced with mock pride.

I laughed, watching him take a sip of coffee. "I didn't think I'd see the day you traded stadium lights for a frying pan."

"Balance," he said easily. "It keeps me grounded." Then, glancing at me, he added, "You do that too, you know."

Something about the way he said it made my chest tighten, that small flicker of something both terrifying and good.

Later, we spent the afternoon exploring the city. He drove us through Wynwood, and my gaze swept over streets, alive with color and music. We stopped at a café tucked between murals, where he ordered us strong Cuban coffee and pastries dusted with sugar. I watched him speak Spanish to the barista, and felt the strange comfort of seeing a side of him that didn't belong to the public—not the athlete and the man on ESPN highlights, just Diego. *My* Diego.

He pointed to a mural of a woman's face painted in blues and golds.

"That one's my favorite," he said. "The artist comes back every summer to add a new layer. I like that it changes but never loses itself."

I followed his gaze, smiling. "Like people, I guess. Still the same underneath, just learning to hold more."

He looked at me like I had said something worth remembering. "Yeah," he said quietly. "Exactly like that."

That night, we went to a rooftop restaurant overlooking the water. The city glittered below us, the air soft and warm. Between the laughter and the wine, the conversation deepened—those late-night kinds of talks that pull you closer without even meaning to.

"What about you?" I asked, chin resting in my hand. "What's it really like? Being a professional soccer player. You've told me little bits and pieces that every soccer player says in front of the cameras when we first met, but not the truth behind it."

He leaned back in his chair, eyes thoughtful. "It's a lot of hard work and pressure. I love the roar of the crowd and the rush when the game starts. But it's not all that people think it is. There's loneliness in it, too. You're always somewhere new, surrounded by people, but missing the ones who make you feel like yourself."

I reached across the table and brushed my fingers against his hand. "I get that. Being a mom and having a job that takes so much of me makes me feel like I'm always balancing between what I need to do and what I want to feel."

He turned his palm up, threading our fingers together. "Maybe that's why we found each other. We both live between the lines ... responsibility and freedom, dreams and real life."

I nodded. "Maybe so."

By Sunday morning, my suitcase sat by the door, and he lingered in every doorway I passed.

"Do you really have to leave?" he asked.

"If I don't, I might never go back." A small smile curved my lips. I didn't want to leave either, but what choice did I have?

"Would that be so bad?" he teased, though his eyes said something deeper.

"Probably not," I said, "but I'd eventually have to face reality."

He wrapped his arms around me, his chin resting against my hair. "Then at least promise you'll come back."

"I promise."

The ride to the airport was mostly spent in silence, where both of us just enjoyed each other's presence. There, he parked the car and walked me to the gate even though he didn't have to. We stood there for a long time, caught between words and silence.

"I'll return the favor soon," he said finally, a faint smile tugging at his mouth. "Next time, I'll be the one flying to Houston."

He brushed his thumb along my jaw before leaning in, his lips finding mine in a kiss that felt slow and unhurried, like the world could wait a little longer. It was difficult to pry myself away from him, but I would have missed my plane otherwise.

As the plane climbed higher, Miami stretched out below me—blue and golden and full of memories I wasn't ready to let go of. I leaned my forehead against the window, still tasting him on my lips. It was the one taste I didn't want to ever forget.

Weeks slipped by in fragments—airports and goodbyes, messages that started with *good morning* and ended with *miss you already.*

The rhythm of us became its own kind of routine. He'd text me pictures of morning coffee on his balcony, and I'd send photos of Sophie making a mess of pancake batter. Between the distance, we carved out small pockets of connection—stolen minutes that somehow kept us tethered.

Every time his name lit up my phone, my stomach fluttered with butterflies. This wasn't just a passing thing anymore—it had roots, even if they were stretched across states. But there was one thing I couldn't ignore: He had not met Sophie.

At first, it made sense to keep things separate. I wanted to be sure—to protect her, and to protect myself, too. But after nearly three months of this, it started to feel like waiting was its own kind of fear. One evening, I called him.

"Diego, I want you to meet her," I told him the moment he picked up.

He paused. "Sophie?"

I nodded, even though he couldn't see me. "I've been holding back, but she's, my world. If you're going to be part of my life, you have to meet her, too."

There was a moment of quiet before his voice came through. I could practically hear him smile as he spoke. "I'd be honored." And just like that, the line I'd drawn between my heart and my life began to blur.

When he came to Houston, the air was thick with July heat. Sophie met him at the door with cautious curiosity, clutching her favorite stuffed bear by one arm. I'd told her that Diego was special to me, and she had also agreed she wanted to meet him. Still, now, looking at her in her blue dotted dress, I wondered if I had made a decision too rashly and was introducing them too soon.

Diego crouched immediately, meeting her at eye level.

"Hey there," he said gently, his accent softening the words. "Who's this little guy?"

Sophie narrowed her eyes in mock suspicion. "This is Mr. Buttons. He doesn't talk to strangers."

Diego's lips twitched into a grin. "That's fair. Maybe if I tell him a secret, he'll change his mind."

She blinked, clearly intrigued. "Depends on the secret."

He leaned closer and whispered something into Mr. Button's ear. Sophie's mouth fell open in delight.

"What did you say?" she demanded.

"I told him I flew all the way here just to meet the two most important people in Houston."

She giggled, shaking her head. "That's not a secret!"

"Maybe not," Diego said, standing up with a grin. "But it's still true."

Her shoulders relaxed, the wall between them gone in an instant. She handed him the bear. "Okay. You can sit next to us at dinner."

"Deal," he said, accepting Mr. Buttons like it was the most serious promise in the world. Watching them together felt surreal—like two pieces of my world had just clicked into place. I had never thought I'd let someone not only in my life, but also hers. Yet here we were.

Over dinner, Sophie did most of the talking, telling Diego about her favorite movies, her best friend, and how she was teaching herself to whistle. Diego listened intently, nodding and asking questions, never once checking his phone or glancing away.

I watched quietly, memorizing the small, ordinary miracle of it—the ease, the laughter, and the way Sophie leaned into him like she had known him longer than an evening. It just felt so natural.

After dinner, the three of us sat on the porch. The air hummed with cicadas, warm and alive. Sophie leaned against Diego's arm, peppering him with questions faster than he could answer, and he met every one with patience and humor.

When I tucked her into bed later, she blinked up at me, sleep already pulling her under.

"He's nice, Mommy," she murmured, clutching Mr. Buttons. "He talks like a movie person."

I laughed softly. "Yeah. He kind of does."

Back outside, Diego stood by the railing, the glow from the porch light catching the edges of his hair.

"She's incredible," he said quietly. "You've done such a good job with her."

I joined him, leaning beside him. "Thank you. I was terrified to let anyone near this part of my life, but I don't regret tonight the slightest bit. It went better than I could have ever imagined."

He turned to me, his eyes steady. "I get it. But thank you for letting me try."

And that's when I knew—I wasn't just letting him in. I was letting myself trust.

Eleven
Amelia

Summer didn't happen all at once; it crept in on ordinary days, and we made a home out of them.

Most weekends, Diego flew to Houston. He'd text me his arrival time with a plane emoji, like it was a private joke, then show up at my door with something small for Sophie: a tiny dolphin, a sparkly sticker sheet, a paperback about constellations he said he'd read as a kid. She'd pretend not to care, then sleep with it clutched in her hand. Mr. Buttons tolerated the competition.

We learned each other's rhythms without trying. He liked his coffee too strong; I always forgot my mug in the microwave. He folded dish towels the "wrong" way and turned all my cereal boxes so the labels faced the same direction. He burned pancakes once, then made a second batch so perfect Sophie proclaimed him "pancake champion" and fashioned a foil crown.

Nights were easy. After Sophie's bath and a story, sometimes he did the voices, and she laughed so hard she hiccuped, we'd drift to the porch. The cicadas continued to hum through the summer. Heat pressed softly against our skin. He'd sit close, knee against mine, and tell me about the quiet parts of his life I wouldn't find in a headline: the ache in his left ankle when rain was coming, the way he always counted steps before a corner kick, and the field he trained on as a teenager, which still smelled like cut grass and summers that felt endless.

I told him the small things, too—how Sophie said "ambulance" with the "b" on purpose because she liked the sound. How I never outgrew the habit of checking the door twice. How sometimes the view from my window made me feel proud and lonely at the same time. He listened like there wasn't anywhere else to be. That was the startling part, how peaceful it felt to be heard.

By late August, the edges of that peace started to shimmer. His phone buzzed more in the mornings. There were emails with subject lines such as "Media Day" and "Training Block." He didn't talk about it much, but I caught the look on his face sometimes, present and far at once, like part of him was already lacing up his boots.

One Friday, I found him sitting cross-legged on the living room rug while Sophie arranged a tea party with serious ceremony. He held the tiniest cup between his thumb and forefinger.

"Would Mr. Buttons prefer lemon or cloud milk?" he asked.

"Both," Sophie declared, "obviously." I leaned in the doorway and watched something in my chest loosen and ache at the same time.

Later, after we tucked her in, he traced the inside of my wrist with his thumb and said, "I wish this could stay exactly like this."

"I know," I said. I didn't ask *how* it would. I already knew he didn't have the answer any more than I did.

The following week, his schedule became more crowded. Two days' notice turned into one. A Sunday flight became a Saturday night. "I'll make it up to you," he said, and he meant it, but meaning things and managing them were cousins, not twins.

That was when I decided to go to Miami, one last weekend before preseason swallowed him whole. Sophie would stay with my parents; she was thrilled at the prospect of pancakes for dinner and a movie "with snacks not in bowls." My mom raised an eyebrow when I asked.

"You sure?" she said, but there was a softness under it. I nodded. She squeezed my hand.

"Yeah," I told her with a slight nod, "I'm sure." When I told Diego, he sent three messages in a row.

Diego:
Are you serious?

Diego:
You just made my entire week.

Diego:
I'm picking you up. No arguments.

Me:
Not arguing. Just tell me what kind of coffee to bring for your bribe.

He replied with a pin to his favorite café and a voice note full of laughter.

Diego:
Bring yourself. Everything else is extra.

For the first time in days, the air around me felt light again. I closed my laptop, set my phone face down, and stood a minute in the kitchen, listening to the house breathe. It wasn't that I believed a weekend could solve the season coming. I just wanted a pocket of time that belonged to us before the calendar was everyone else's.

I packed light. Summer clothes, the dress he'd said made my eyes look like "trouble," sandals, and the necklace Sophie calls my "good luck moon." I tucked a crayon drawing into the pocket of my tote, Sophie's stick-figure portrait of "Me, Mom, D," with Mr. Buttons floating above us like a zeppelin. When she handed it to me, she'd said, "So you don't forget." As if forgetting had ever been the risk.

On the morning of my flight, she held my hand all the way to the car, our steps out of sync and perfect. "Tell Diego I said hi," she ordered, in a serious tone. "And tell him I want my crown back."

"What crown?" I asked, buckling her into the booster.

"The pancake champion one," she said, as if I were slow. "It's a loan."

I kissed her forehead. "Duly noted."

At the curb, my mom hugged me too long and whispered, "Enjoy it. And take your time."

"I'll be back Sunday," I said, but I knew she didn't mean the logistics. I knew she meant the moment.

As I walked toward security, my phone buzzed.

Diego:

At arrivals. Can't wait to see you.

Me:

Be there soon.

Diego:

Hurry. Before I embarrass myself and start grinning at strangers.

I did hurry. And for the first time since the emails started stacking up and the mornings got shorter, I felt like we were stepping toward the same thing.

Miami, one last weekend before the season, I repeated it in my head like a promise I was making to both of us: we'd hold this, and then we'd see.

The Miami air was thick with heat, the kind that clings to your skin and made the city feel alive. I spotted Diego the moment I stepped out of baggage claim, leaning against his car, cap pulled low, hands in his pockets. Even in the chaos of travelers and rolling suitcases, he stood out effortlessly.

He saw me before I could wave. That smile was all it took for everything inside me to settle. "You made it," he said as I reached him.

"I told you I would," I teased, and he bent down to kiss the side of my head, his hand finding the small of my back as if it belonged there.

"You always keep your promises," he murmured, and somehow that simple sentence made my heart ache.

He drove with the windows down, wind tangling my hair as the ocean came into view. The city was alive around us, music spilling from cafés and palm trees flashing by in streaks of green and gold. Our fingers brushed on the console until his hand found mine completely, his thumb tracing lazy circles over my skin.

We stopped at a small café tucked on a corner where the scent of espresso drifted into the street. "Best Cuban coffee in the city," he said confidently.

I took a sip and nearly choked. "That's ... strong."

He laughed, that deep, warm laugh that made me forget there was anyone else around. "You'll thank me later."

"Doubtful," I said, even as I took another sip.

The day passed in easy rhythm, strolling along the beach, sharing bites of fresh fruit, and watching the waves crash against the shore as he told me stories about his early days playing soccer barefoot on cracked pavement. By evening, we'd changed and were heading to a quiet coastal restaurant he loved, tucked near the marina.

Inside, warm light spilled over the tables, the air alive with soft chatter and the scent of grilled fish and citrus. It was supposed to be discreet, but as soon as we walked in, a few heads turned.

At first, I thought I was imagining the double takes and the murmured whispers, but then a group of teenage boys practically sprinted over, phones already out.

"Yo, no way ... Diego Álvarez?!" one of them shouted, eyes wide. "Bro, you're going to *kill it* this season!"

Another one jumped in, breathless. "Dude, that goal against L.A.? That was unreal! You're a machine!"

Diego laughed, easy and good-natured, signing a napkin before they all crowded in for a selfie. "You guys ready for kick-off?" he asked, crouching slightly so they could fit in the frame.

They started talking over each other, fantasy teams, match predictions, someone yelling, "You're my captain every week, bro!"

Finally, one of them blurted, "You're a legend, man!" before they jogged off, still buzzing and shouting his name.

I stood a few feet back, watching it all unfold. The way he carried himself—so calm, so present—wasn't because of his ego. It was because of love. He genuinely loved what he did, and the joy of it radiated from him, softening something inside me.

When he turned back to me, cheeks slightly pink, he said, "Sorry about that."

"Don't be." I smiled. "They adore you. And I get it."

He tilted his head, amusement glinting in his eyes. "You get it, huh?"

"Yeah. You're impossible not to root for."

That made him laugh, and he reached for my hand as the host led us to our table by the window. "Good," he murmured, fingers brushing mine. "Because I'm rooting for us."

Dinner was quiet in the best way—warm light, clinking glasses, and the sound of the ocean just beyond the open windows. We ordered grilled snapper and a bottle of wine that Diego insisted was 'just enough to feel like vacation.'

"So," I said, swirling my glass, "does that happen often? People recognizing you like that?"

He chuckled. "Sometimes. Mostly after big matches. Miami's a smaller world than people think—you run into fans everywhere."

"They love you," I said. "You can tell."

He leaned back, the candlelight catching the curve of his jaw. "I love the game. The rest comes with it." He paused, looking at me. "It's weird, though. They see the goals and the press. They don't see the travel, the noise, and the pressure. It's a lot."

I studied him, the edge of honesty in his tone softening his usual confidence. "And now preseason's starting soon," I said quietly.

"Next week," he admitted, exhaling. "Once that kicks in, it's nonstop. Early mornings, late flights, media obligations. It's like being swallowed whole."

I felt my chest tighten a little. "You sound like you're already missing it."

He shook his head, his hand brushing mine across the table. "I'm not. I'm just trying to be realistic. This, he motioned between us, "means something to me. You mean something to me. But once the season starts, things get harder. Calls, visits, time … it all becomes more complicated." His words were steady but tinged with something vulnerable, like he wanted to warn me without pushing me away. "I'm ready for it if you are."

"I know," I said, my voice softer than I intended. "I don't need perfect. I just need honesty."

He smiled faintly, thumb tracing the edge of my hand. "Then I can do that."

We didn't talk about schedules after that. Instead, he told me stories about his first club in Spain, the way he used to sneak onto empty fields as a kid to feel the grass under his shoes. I told him about more about Sophie, my everlasting source of stories, how she hated carrots, and how she'd once cut her own bangs because she wanted to "see like mommy." He laughed so hard at that one he nearly spilled his drink.

And for a while, it was easy again.

Just us.

After dinner, we walked along the boardwalk. Music drifted from a nearby bar, soft and romantic. He slid his arm around my waist, and I leaned into him, memorizing the weight of that moment, the smell of the ocean, the rhythm of our steps, the unspoken ache of knowing it wouldn't last forever.

"Promise me something," he said suddenly.

"What's that?"

"That you won't forget this when things get crazy. When I'm buried in travel or games or press, and I can't call as much as I want to—remember this, okay?"

I nodded, my throat tight. "Only if you promise to do the same."

He stopped walking then, turning to face me under the glow of the streetlight. "Deal," he whispered before kissing me, slow and steady, as the night hummed around us.

***

The next morning came too quickly.

Sunlight spilled across the sheets, warm and golden, but instead of feeling peaceful, it pressed against me with the heaviness of goodbye.

Diego was quiet as we packed. Every movement felt slower, his hand folding my shirt carefully, my suitcase clicking shut with a soft finality neither of us wanted to face.

When we reached the airport, the city already felt different. The noise seemed sharper, the air heavier. He parked and insisted on walking me inside, even though I told him he didn't have to. *Again.*

"You'll miss your training debrief meeting," I said.

"I'll survive," he replied, that half-smile tugging at his lips.

Inside, the terminal buzzed with people rushing around us, vacationers, families, and business travelers. For a moment, it felt like we were standing still in a world that was moving too fast.

He reached for my bag, his fingers brushing mine. "I hate this part."

"I know." I swallowed hard, forcing a smile. "But it's just a few weeks."

"Until the season starts," he said quietly. "Then everything changes again."

I met his gaze. "It doesn't have to."

He looked at me then the way he always did right before he kissed me, like he was memorizing me, piece by piece. "You make it sound simple."

"Maybe it is," I said softly. "We just try."

He nodded slowly, then pulled me closer. The noise around us faded until it was just the rhythm of his breath, the faint brush of his thumb against my cheek.

"I love you, Amelia," he said suddenly, the words slipping out before either of us could stop them. It was the first time either of us had said it. My breath caught. His voice was steady, but there was a tremor underneath, like he'd been holding it in.

"I love you, too," I whispered, my heart pounding in my chest.

He looked me in the eyes and kissed me then, slow, certain, and deep enough that I felt it in my bones. It wasn't rushed or desperate. It was the kind of kiss that said, *'I'll wait.'*

When he pulled back, his forehead rested against mine. "Go before I follow you through security," he murmured.

I smiled through the ache. "Don't tempt me."

He chuckled, but his hand stayed on my waist until the last possible second. As I stepped into the security line, I glanced back. He was still there, hands in his pockets, eyes on me, that same soft, unguarded smile that had undone me from the start.

When I landed, I spotted Sophie before she saw me, pink backpack, curls flying, waving both hands.

"Mommy!"

I dropped my bag, catching her mid-run. Her laughter hit me like sunlight.

"There's my girl," I whispered, kissing her cheek. "Did you have fun with Nana?"

"We went to the zoo," she said proudly. "And Nana let me get ice cream before dinner!"

I glanced up at my mom, who was smiling like she'd gotten away with something.

"She's impossible to say no to," she said, taking Sophie's hand. "How was Miami?"

"It was good," I said, smiling softly. "Really good."

My mom gave a knowing look but didn't push. "I'm glad. You needed a break."

We walked to the car, Sophie chattering the entire way, and for the first time since boarding the plane, I let myself exhale. The world had steadied, but something in me hadn't.

Back home, after dinner and bedtime routines, the quiet hit me. The hum of the dishwasher. The faint sound of crickets outside. The kind of silence that feels too loud. I was on my own again. I curled up on the couch, scrolling absently before finally opening our messages.

Me:

Made it home safe, babe. I miss you already.

It didn't take long for the typing bubbles to appear.

Diego:

I'm glad you made it back safe. I miss you too, amor.

I smiled, my chest tightening.

Me:

Good luck with pre-season training tomorrow. Don't overdo it.

Diego:

I'll try. No promises. You know how I am.

Me:

Stubborn.

Diego:

Dedicated. ;)

Me:

Call it what you want. Just don't forget about me when the chaos starts.

Diego:

Never. You're my favorite distraction.

I laughed quietly, shaking my head as I typed back a goodnight message. For a few minutes, I lay there smiling at the ceiling, the ache of missing him wrapped in something warm and hopeful.

But time always had a way of changing things.

Two weeks passed in flashes of early alarms, work deadlines, and school drop-offs. Diego and I still texted every day, but the rhythm was different now. Where there used to be long conversations and late-night calls, there were quick check-ins between his practices and recovery sessions.

Diego:

Long day. Heading to bed
early. Miss you amor

Me:

Sweet dreams. Rest up. Proud of you.

Sometimes he'd reply hours later, sometimes not until the next morning. The emojis were still there, but something underneath felt muted. I stared at the photo booth photos that were pinned to my fridge with a magnet. Somehow, they only made me miss him more.

By the end of the second week, I caught myself checking my phone too often, rereading old messages to feel close to him again. It wasn't that he'd disappeared, he hadn't. He was just ... quieter.

And for someone like me, who had spent years learning not to need too much, that silence pressed against something I'd worked hard to protect.

By Friday night, the quiet between us had turned into something heavier.

It wasn't that Diego stopped reaching out; he just seemed to exist somewhere farther away now. His messages were shorter, his tone softer but distant, like his mind was always halfway on the field.

I tried to tell myself it was just preseason, and that once he found his rhythm again, things would settle.

But when the third "*Sorry, long day, call you tomorrow*" text came and went with no call the next night either, I finally caved and opened the group chat.

Anastasia:

Okay, I know that silence. You've got the "guy acting weird" face, don't you?

Victoria:

Spill it. What's going on with Mr. Soccer Star? You've been quiet all week.

I hesitated, fingers hovering over the screen. Then I typed what I didn't want to say out loud.

Me:

He's … off. We still talk, but it's different. Slower. Like something's changed, and I can't tell if it's just him being busy or if I'm losing him already.

Anastasia:

Is this about the preseason thing starting? Didn't he say it'd be intense for a bit?

Me:

Yeah, but it feels like he's slipping away. We went from texting all day to maybe a handful of messages. I know he's tired, but I just … I miss him.

Victoria:

Oh, babe. You're not crazy for feeling that. Long distance is hard, even when it's good. But don't start pulling away before he does. Communicate.

Anastasia:

And don't jump to conclusions either. You know how guys get tunnel vision when they're focused. Especially athletes.

Victoria:

True, but that doesn't mean she should sit there wondering. You deserve effort, even if he's busy.

Their messages blinked across the screen, back-to-back. Both were right, and both were saying things I'd been arguing with myself about for days.

Me:

I don't want to sound needy.

Anastasia:

Needy? Girl, you let him into your life, into Sophie's world. You're not asking for too much. You're asking for consistency.

Victoria:

Exactly. Just talk to him, Amelia. If it's real, he'll listen.

I sighed, reading their messages over and over. They made it sound easy. For them, maybe it was. For me, saying what I felt always came with risk—the risk of being too much or not enough.

Still, they were right.

If I wanted this to work, I had to stop protecting myself from something that hadn't even happened yet.

I clicked open Diego's chat and started typing.

Me:

> Hey, love. I hope everything's okay. I know preseason's crazy right now, but I've been missing you a lot. It just feels like something's shifted between us lately, and I don't know if it's just me overthinking or if you feel it too. I'm not trying to add pressure — I just want to make sure we're okay.

The message hovered there for a moment before I hit send. Minutes turned into an hour. Then two. I told myself he was tired, asleep, overwhelmed. But the silence was loud enough to drown out every excuse. The next morning came and went before his name finally lit up my screen.

Diego:

> Hey, amor. I'm sorry if I've seemed distant. Things have been nonstop with training, and I've been feeling overwhelmed. It's not you, I promise. I care about you, a lot. I just need to get through this week, okay?

Relief came first. Then frustration.

Me:

> I understand. Just don't forget I'm here, okay?

The typing bubble appeared. Then disappeared. And the silence settled again.

By the third night, I couldn't take it anymore. The house was still. The only sound was the hum of the refrigerator and the soft tick of the clock above the sink. I sat at the kitchen table, staring at his last message, thumb tracing the edge of my phone. My gaze drifted to the fridge, where our smiling selves were still trapped in time.

I told myself not to call and to wait, but waiting had started to feel like its own kind of heartbreak. I hit dial before I could stop myself.

He answered on the second ring, voice soft, like he'd been thinking of me too. "Hey. I was just about to text you."

"Were you?"

"Of course. I know I've been quiet, "

"I get that you're busy," I said, cutting him off gently, fingers tightening around my coffee mug. "But it feels different. *You* feel different. And I don't know what to do with that."

He exhaled, the sound heavy through the line. "I'm not pulling away. I care about you. But the preseason's rough this year. My head's been all over the place."

"I understand," I said softly. "I really do. But I need to know where I fit in that. I don't want to feel like I'm waiting for someone who's already gone."

"You're not waiting for nothing. I just need to focus right now. This season matters. And I hate that it means I can't give you everything you deserve." His honesty hit harder than denial ever could.

"I'm not asking for everything," I said. "Just to feel like I still matter, even when things get hard. Like we said, remember?"

"You do matter, *amor*," he said, almost instantly. "You and Sophie both. Tell her I miss her, okay?"

I blinked back the sting in my eyes. "I will."

Neither of us spoke after that. The quiet between us was full of things we didn't know how to fix.

"I think we both need a little space," I said finally. "Just to breathe. Figure out what this looks like now that life's speeding up again."

He hesitated, then sighed. "I don't want to lose you, Amelia."

"I don't want to lose you either," I whispered. "But I can't be the only one to feel like I'm holding us together."

"Then one day at a time," he said softly. "That's all I can promise right now."

"One day at a time," I repeated.

Twelve
Diego

Mexico heat hit different.

It was the kind that stuck to your lungs, heavy and unforgiving, the kind that reminded you how small you were under the sun.

We'd been here a week for preseason, two-a-days, press obligations, and endless drills, and my body had already given up pretending it wasn't exhausted.

Training started at sunrise, the air thick with humidity and the smell of cut grass. The coaches didn't care about your personal life, if your mind wandered, they'd drag you back into focus fast.

"Alvarez, pick it up!"

"Move your feet, again!"

By the third day, my body felt like it had been wrung out.

Still, between drills, I checked my phone. Messages from Amelia popped up in short bursts:

Amelia:
How's training? You surviving?

Amelia:
Miss you.

I'd type responses in my head, but by the time I had a free second, exhaustion always won. I told myself I'd reply properly later, and later never came soon enough.

After training, in the locker room, Taije and Luka sat beside me, talking about the upcoming season. Luka was new, young, fast, still had that hungry edge.

"Yo, Alvarez," Taije said, kicking my shin lightly. "You look like someone stole your phone and your soul with it."

"Yeah," Luka chimed in, grinning. "He's been checking that thing like it owes him money."

I smirked, rubbing the back of my neck. "Just someone I care about."

Taije raised a brow. "Amelia?"

"Yeah," I said quietly. There was no one else for me.

Luka whistled. "The one from Vegas?"

"Yeah."

Taije leaned back against the lockers. "Didn't you meet her kid, too? Sophie, right? Man, that's serious."

"It's different," I admitted. "I've done long distance before, but this—" I shook my head. "I'm not used to caring about someone who has more to lose than I do."

Taije studied me. "You sound scared."

"I am." It came out before I could stop it. "I don't want to let her down. But if I lose focus here, everything I've built—my career, it all falls apart. And I can't be that guy who makes promises and breaks them."

Luka kicked at the bench, his voice softer now. "Maybe she doesn't need promises. Just some reassurance."

I nodded, but the words didn't stick, that was the thing no one told you about love when you lived like this, when your days were spent under stadium lights and your nights in empty hotel rooms. You could care about someone deeply and still fail to show up in the way they need. And I hated knowing that might already be happening.

By the end of the first week, the exhaustion was bone-deep. We'd train until sundown, eat, review film, and sleep. Repeat.

I'd text her when I could, but my messages got shorter, fewer. I could see it happening, even as I tried to fight it. Then came her text, the one that hit harder than any tackle I'd ever taken.

Amelia:

Hey, love. I know we said we'd take it one day at a time, but I just wanted you to know I'm still thinking of you. Hope all is going well x

I stared at it for a long time, my thumb hovering, heart in my throat. She wasn't wrong. Something had shifted—but not in the way she thought.

It wasn't distance. It was fear. Fear of losing her. Fear of not being enough. Fear that the life I'd built, the one I'd spent years perfecting, didn't have space for the kind of love she deserved.

I typed slowly, replying. It felt hollow the second I sent it, like trying to fix a fracture with tape.

Later that night, I lay in bed, muscles screaming, the glow of my phone lighting the ceiling. I thought about Amelia in her apartment, the soft hum of Houston outside her window, and Sophie asleep down the hall. I thought about how she'd look at her phone, waiting. I wanted to call her to tell her everything, but words felt too small for what I was trying to balance.

So, I just whispered into the dark, "I'm trying, *amor*. I'm still here." And I hoped, wherever she was, she still believed me.

Thirteen
Amelia

After the call with Diego two weeks ago, I'd thrown myself back into work. It was easier that way—less time to dwell on the gaps in our conversations, and less time to wonder what might happen next. I needed the distraction, and Elite Source provided plenty. Today was no different.

I walked into the office, greeted by the familiar rush of activity. The scent of coffee hung in the air, mingling with the quiet hum of productivity. Lisa popped her head around the corner, her bright smile as infectious as ever.

"Morning, Amelia! How was your weekend?" she asked, her eyes sparkling with curiosity.

"Hey, Lisa. It was good, I just spent time with Sophie and caught up on some things around the house. How about you?"

"Same old, same old," she said with a shrug, then held out a file. "Oh, and don't forget, we've got that big meeting later on the new makeup brand campaign."

I nodded, taking the file from her and sinking into my chair. The familiar routine of reviewing proposals and shaping marketing strategies wrapped around me like a comforting blanket. Work was my sanctuary, a place where I could channel my energy and avoid the uncertainty that lingered outside these walls.

It had been two weeks since that phone call with Diego. We'd talked here and there—quick texts and brief check-ins, but nothing deep that felt like we were moving forward. Maybe that was why I buried myself in this project, focusing all my attention on the upcoming launch. I could control this. I could make this campaign a success. But Diego? That was a different story.

I was reviewing the campaign's creative assets when my phone buzzed on the desk. Without thinking, I glanced at the screen and saw his name.

Diego:

Hey, I've got a break from training this weekend. Would love to see you. How about I come to Houston?

My heart stuttered. For a moment, I just stared at the message, my mind racing. We hadn't seen each other in weeks, and now he wanted to come here? I wasn't sure if I was ready for that. Was I ready to open myself up again, to let him back into my space when things between us still felt so ... unresolved?

I tapped my fingers on the edge of my desk, staring at the screen as if the words would change. Part of me wanted to say yes, to jump at the chance to spend time with him again. But the other part of me—the cautious part—was hesitant. Could we really make this work long-distance? Or was I setting myself up to get hurt again?

"Everything okay?" Lisa's voice broke into my thoughts, and I looked up to find her eyeing me with concern.

"Yeah, just … Diego. He wants to come to Houston this weekend."

Her eyes widened. "Oh, really? Are you going to see him?"

I hesitated, weighing the options in my head. "I don't know yet. We'll see."

Lisa gave me an understanding nod. "Well, whatever you decide, just make sure it's what you want, not what you feel like you should do."

I smiled, appreciating her advice. She had a point. I needed to figure out what I wanted, not just react to Diego's moves. This wasn't just about his schedule or his wants—it had to be about what I needed too.

As I turned my attention back to the campaign, Diego's message lingered in the back of my mind. I wanted to see him, that was for sure, but that was the less logical part of me, one that wanted to follow my heart. I needed to be rational about this, though.

As Lisa and I sat down for lunch, the chatter of the office cafeteria hummed around us, but my mind was somewhere else. I poked at my salad absentmindedly, hoping to distract myself with work thoughts, but it wasn't working. Lisa was already eyeing me, as if she could sense my unease.

"So, what's the update on Diego?" Lisa asked, her tone gentle but direct. She never beat around the bush when she could tell something was up.

I sighed, leaning back in my chair. "It's been a couple of weeks since that phone call. We've talked here and there, but it feels off, you know? Like there's this distance growing, even when we do talk." I hadn't even responded yet—since I didn't know what to say, still.

She paused mid-bite. "And this morning? Have you spoken to him about him visiting?"

"I just don't know if I should," I admitted. "I don't want to get more attached if it's not going to go anywhere. It's easy to say 'yes' when we're apart, but what happens when we see each other again, and it's still the same struggle?"

Lisa rested her sandwich down; her brow furrowed in concern. "I get why you're cautious, but if he's asking to come out here, doesn't that mean something? He's making the effort. I mean, maybe seeing him in person again will clear some of these doubts you're having."

"I just don't want to get hurt. What if it's just more of the same?" I said, feeling the frustration bubble up. "What if he's here, but he's still distant? And then I've let him back in just to feel that all over again?"

She smiled softly, leaning forward. "That's fair. But how can you know if you don't see him? I think you owe it to yourself to find out. If he's willing to come all the way here, that's something, right? Give him a chance to show you where his head's at."

I sighed, not entirely convinced but appreciating her logic. "I know. It's just scary, you know? The idea of investing in something that might not work."

"Of course it is," Lisa said, her voice kind. "But you've been handling so much—work, Sophie, everything. Maybe you can let him handle this one. You're always the one holding it together; maybe it's time to let him put in the work. It doesn't have to be all on you."

Her words settled in, and I couldn't help but smile a little. "Maybe you're right. I just … I guess I'm afraid of putting too much hope into something that could let me down."

"That's normal," she said. "But give him the chance to prove himself. He might surprise you."

I nodded, still unsure but feeling lighter. "Thanks, Lisa. I needed to hear that."

I stared at my phone again, the weight of her words sinking in. She was right. I couldn't keep putting it off, waiting for the perfect moment or clear answer. I had to take a step, make a move. Diego was making the effort to come to me … maybe I needed to meet him halfway.

Taking a deep breath, I opened the message and typed, my heart racing with each word.

Me:

> Okay, I'd love to see you this weekend. Let me know your plans.

I hit send before I could overthink it any further. There, it was done. A small part of me felt relieved, while the rest of me was bracing for what came next.

Lisa smiled, noticing the shift in my expression. "There you go. Now let him take the next step."

"Yeah," I said, feeling a mix of hope and fear swirl inside me. "Now we'll see."

Fourteen

Amelia

I paced back and forth across the living room, my heart tapping a nervous rhythm against my ribs. Diego would be arriving any minute, and I couldn't tell if the flutter in my stomach was excitement or panic … or both.

Sophie sat curled up on the couch, her legs swinging humming softly as she colored. The late afternoon sun filtered through the blinds, painting faint golden stripes across her cheeks.

"Mommy, when's Nana coming?" she asked, glancing up with her big, curious eyes.

"She'll be here soon, sweetie," I said, trying to sound calm as I smoothed the skirt of my dress for the third time. My hands wouldn't stay still. I hadn't seen Diego in weeks, and tonight carried an odd blend of hope and uncertainty that made my chest ache. "Nana is going to watch you while Mommy has dinner with Diego."

"Oh! You're going on a date?" she teased, grinning. "Wait, why can't I come with you?"

Her question stopped me cold. There was such an innocent eagerness in her voice that it tugged at me. I knew she missed him, too. Diego had made an impression, the kind that a child of her age wouldn't forget easily.

"You'll see him soon, I promise," I said softly, crouching down so we were eye to eye. "We just have to talk about some things first, okay?"

She tilted her head, lips curling with mischief. "Does that mean you're going to kiss him?"

I laughed, a nervous sound escaping me as I tucked a loose strand of hair behind my ear. "Maybe, maybe not. We'll see."

"Ew!" she squealed, but her giggles filled the room, shaking off the tension that had been wrapped around me all day. A knock sounded at the door, The two of us stared at each other for a moment before she made a move.

"That's him!" Sophie jumped up before I could move, excitement lighting up her little face. "Can I open it?"

"Not yet, sweetheart," I said, wiping my palms on my dress before crossing the room. I took a small breath before opening the door to find Diego standing there, sunlight spilling over his shoulders, and a relaxed smile tugging at his lips. He was dressed in jeans and a simple white t-shirt.

"Hey," he said, his gaze washing over me. "You look beautiful."

Before I could even respond, Sophie peeked out from behind my leg. "Diego!" she squealed, her entire face lighting up.

His expression softened instantly. "Hey, *pequeñita*," he said, crouching down to her level. "You've gotten taller! What have you been eating, huh?"

"Chicken nuggets," she said proudly. "Mom says it's not healthy, but I like them."

Diego laughed, and something inside me melted at the sound. Watching him with her, so natural, so gentle, was almost too much. I already knew it'd make the distance even harder to handle.

"Nana is taking me to stay with her tonight," Sophie announced. "Mommy said you're taking her on a date."

Diego shot me a teasing glance, eyes glinting. "Oh, she did, did she?"

Before I could answer, another knock came, this time lighter, and more familiar. My mom didn't bother to wait for me to open the door, though. Instead, she stepped in with her usual bright smile, holding a bag of snacks and books.

"Hi, honey. Oh, " she paused as her eyes landed on Diego.

I took a steadying breath. This wasn't exactly how I imagined their first meeting would go, but it was as good as any. It would have to do. "Mom, this is Diego."

Her smile widened. "So, this is the famous Diego," she said warmly, extending her hand. "I've heard plenty."

"Good things, I hope," he said, shaking her hand with the easy charm that made people instantly like him.

"Mostly," my mom teased, and I stared in sheer horror. Thankfully, neither of them seemed to take any of this seriously. "Nice to finally meet you."

Sophie piped up, "Nana, Diego says chicken nuggets make you tall."

"Oh, does he now?" my mom said, chuckling as she set her bag down.

The small exchange eased the tension I hadn't realized was building. It felt right. Comfortable.

"Well," I said, glancing between them, "I should let these two get settled."

Sophie tugged on Diego's sleeve. "Are you coming back later?"

He smiled, resting a hand gently on her shoulder. "You bet I am. Maybe next time we can all go for ice cream, yeah?"

Her face lit up like it was Christmas morning. "Promise?"

"Promise," he said, and the sincerity in his tone made my heart twist.

As I grabbed my purse, my mom gave me a look, one that said more than words ever could. *Approval.* "Have fun, sweetie," she said. "We've got everything covered here."

I bent down to kiss Sophie's forehead. "Be good, okay? And save me a story for when I get home."

"I will! Bye, Mommy. Bye, Diego!" she called, waving as we stepped outside. Diego wrapped his arm around my waist, looking down at me.

"Let's go," he murmured, "I can't wait to spend the rest of the evening with you."

The night outside felt still, almost suspended in time, but inside the restaurant, everything was charged, alive with unspoken words and tension between us. The soft glow of the candlelight flickered across Diego's face, accentuating the sharp angles of his jawline and the intensity in his eyes.

The gap we had been living with these past few weeks was closing, but not without a cost. My body was attuned to his every move and every breath. The air between us felt thick, like gravity had shifted and drawn us toward one another, yet I remained tethered to the doubts that had been quietly festering in the back of my mind.

Diego leaned forward, his forearms resting on the table, his hand reaching out to trace the back of my hand gently. The heat of his touch sent a jolt of electricity through me.

"I have so many things I want to tell you," Diego said at last, his voice low but sure. "But there's one that lingers in my mind more than all the others. Being away from you messes with my head." I met his gaze, and his eyes darkened, a storm of emotions swirling behind them. His vulnerability was written in the lines of his face, in the way his thumb brushed my hand like he needed the contact more than he needed air.

"I know things are hard right now," he continued quietly. "Training has me tied up, and with the season starting soon, it's only going to get busier. I'm not going to lie about that. But every time I'm not on that field, my mind's on you. I can't stop thinking about what we have, about you."

My heart thudded painfully in my chest as his words sank in. There was something different about him tonight, softer, more open, like he'd peeled back a layer I hadn't realized was there before.

"You make me feel like I've got something real. I don't know, I feel grounded around you. I've never felt that way before," he admitted, his voice steady but laced with something fragile. "And I'm done letting the noise of everything else drown that out. I want to show you I can do better. You know, I'm new at this too, letting someone in."

The raw honesty in his tone hit me in a place I hadn't guarded properly. I swallowed hard, my throat thick with emotion. "Diego, I said softly, shaking my head just a little.

"You don't have to be perfect with me. I need to know that when things get hard when you start to pull away again, you'll mean it when you say you want this."

His expression softened, his hand tightening around mine. "I'll show you," he said, voice rough with conviction. "Even when I'm tired. Even when I've got nothing left to give, I'll still show up. These two weeks have shown me that not having you around is more exhausting than anything else in my life."

The sincerity in his voice made my chest tighten, and for a moment, I didn't trust myself to speak. The flicker of candlelight danced across his features, softening him and making him look almost boyish and unguarded. His hand slid up my arm, warm against my skin, and my breath caught as he leaned closer, his gaze dipping to my lips.

"I, " I whispered, my voice trembling. I couldn't find the right words to say everything I wanted to say.

"You don't have to say anything," he murmured, his thumb brushing the side of my neck gently, sending a shiver through me. "Just let me be here. Let me remind you how this feels, how we feel together. I don't want either of us to ever forget it again."

My breath hitched as the space between us disappeared. His lips hovered just inches from mine, his breath warm against my skin. The world outside the restaurant fell away, leaving just the two of us in this charged, intimate moment. The chemistry that had always burned between us ignited again, stronger, more intense than ever.

"I've missed you," I whispered, the emotion breaking through my chest like a wave. His lips finally pressed against mine, soft at first, tentative, as if he was asking permission to show me how much he'd missed me. But then the kiss deepened, urgent and consuming like he couldn't hold back anymore. His hands slid around my waist, pulling me closer as if he needed to feel every inch of me to believe I was really there.

And in that kiss, I could feel everything: his exhaustion, his longing, and his promise to do better. The ache of distance gave way to something fuller, steadier, real.

When we finally pulled apart, both of us were breathless, our foreheads resting against each other. I closed my eyes, letting the moment wash over me, feeling Diego's presence wrap around me.

"Come with me," he whispered against my ear.

"Where?" I asked, barely able to form the word.

"Anywhere. Just stay with me tonight, Amelia. Let me prove to you that this can work."

At that moment, I wanted to believe him. I *needed* to.

"Okay," I whispered, the word escaping before I could stop it. "I'm with you."

Fifteen
Amelia

The cool night air hit my skin as Diego and I stepped outside the restaurant. The quiet hum of the city contrasted with the fire building between us. He took my hand, his fingers threading through mine, and pulled me close as we walked down the street toward his hotel. Every step felt heavier with anticipation, and the tension between us mounted with each glance and each accidental brush of skin.

Before we left, I texted my mom quickly.

Me:

> Hey, Mom, we're going to stay out a bit longer tonight. Thank you for keeping Sophie. I'll grab her in the morning. Love you.

Her reply came almost immediately.

Mom:

> Of course, sweetheart. She's fast asleep.
> Enjoy yourself.

I smiled softly at the screen. My mom always knew when to say the right thing and when to give me space to just be *me*.

When we reached the hotel lobby, the air itself felt charged. I could feel Diego's gaze on me as we waited for the elevator, his hand resting possessively at the small of my back. His touch was gentle, but the hunger behind it was undeniable.

The doors slid open, and we stepped inside. The elevator suddenly felt smaller, the space between us electric. The moment the doors closed, Diego turned toward me, eyes dark with want.

He didn't speak, nor did he need to.

Without a word, he cupped my face, his thumb brushing my cheek. The hum of the elevator blurred into nothing, and the air was thick with anticipation.

"I've been thinking about this moment since the last time I saw you," he murmured, voice low and rough. "All those weeks apart ... this is what got me through them." I couldn't muster a single word under the intensity of his gaze. He leaned in, his lips brushing the corner of my mouth. "I want you," he whispered. "All of you."

The elevator dinged, the doors sliding open to his floor, breaking the moment just long enough for him to pull back, his hand slipping to the small of my back as he led me to his room. The walk down the hallway was a blur, a heady mix of anticipation and desire swirling in the pit of my stomach.

When we reached his door, Diego wasted no time. He swiped the keycard, the door swinging open, and before I could even take in the room, his hands were on me again.

He kicked the door closed behind us, his lips crashing against mine in a kiss that was anything but gentle. It was hungry, demanding, like he had been holding back for too long, and now that we were finally alone, there was no stopping the tidal wave of need between us.

I melted into him, my hands fisting in the fabric of his shirt, pulling him closer as the heat between us flared to life. His hands slid down my back, his fingers pressing into my skin as he deepened the kiss, his tongue tangling with mine in a way that made my knees go weak.

He pulled back, just enough to look at me, his forehead resting against mine as we both tried to catch our breath.

"Tell me you want this," he murmured, his voice rough with emotion. "Tell me you want us."

I stared into his eyes, my chest rising and falling as the weight of his words settled over me. At that moment, there was no doubt and no hesitation. I wanted him—I wanted this.

"I want you," I whispered, my voice barely audible. "I want us."

A slow smile tugged at the corner of his mouth, but the fire in his eyes didn't wane. In one swift motion, he pulled me closer, his hands roaming over my body as he kissed me again, his lips moving with an intensity that made my head spin.

We stumbled toward the bed, our movements a blur of tangled limbs and whispered breaths. My back hit the soft sheets, and Diego hovered over me, his hands framing my face as he gazed down at me with a look that made my heart race.

"I don't want to rush this," he murmured, his thumb brushing over my bottom lip. "I want to take my time with you."

My breath hitched as his words sank in, the heat between us building with every second.

"Then take your time," I whispered, my fingers trailing down his chest, feeling the stiff muscles beneath his shirt.

Diego's eyes darkened with desire, and he leaned down, pressing a soft kiss to the hollow of my throat, his lips tracing a slow, torturous path along my skin. Every touch sent sparks of electricity through me, my body arching into his as the moment's intensity swelled.

He took his time, just like he promised, his hands exploring every inch of my body with reverence, like he was memorizing every curve and every sigh. His lips followed, leaving a trail of heat in their wake, and by the time he finally peeled off my clothes, I was already breathless, trembling beneath his touch.

Before I knew it, he was bare, too, with his shaft prodding against me, teasing me and driving me further into insanity. My lips parted as I forced my hips upward, trying to get him closer to me, but he continued to pull back.

"Please, oh, God, please," I pleaded, and those words seemed to be his undoing. In one rough movement, he slid himself inside me. Now, neither of us could handle teasing or taking it slow any longer, and the way he took me was raw and primal instead. His body slapped against mine with each heavy movement, my nails dragged across his skin, and light sweat coated us both.

And I loved every second of it.

My orgasm hit me sooner than I expected, and it had my entire body tremble as my eyes rolled back into my skull. Somewhere in the distant haze of my brain, I heard his voice again.

"Amelia," he breathed against my skin, his voice thick with emotion. "You have no idea what you do to me."

I didn't respond with words—I couldn't. Instead, I reached up, pulling him down into another searing kiss, pouring every ounce of my desire, my need, into it.

My first wave of pleasure extended into a second, and it wasn't long before he came, too, clutching me as a heavy grunt escaped his lips. I found myself wishing we could stay trapped in that moment forever.

When we finally lay together in the afterglow, our bodies entwined, the room quiet except for the sound of our breathing, Diego pressed a soft kiss to my forehead.

"I meant what I said," he whispered, his voice barely audible in the darkness. "I'm not giving up on us. I don't care how hard it gets."

I smiled against his chest, my heart full in a way it hadn't been in a long time. "Neither am I," I whispered back, and as I closed my eyes, I knew that, no matter what the future held, this was worth fighting for.

I stirred awake to the soft sound of clinking dishes and the tantalizing aroma of freshly brewed coffee wafting through the air. A lazy smile crept onto my face as I blinked against the light, catching sight of Diego balancing a tray laden with breakfast—a perfectly cooked omelet, warm toast, and a small vase holding a single flower.

"Good morning, sleepyhead," he said, a teasing glint in his eye as he set the tray down beside me. The sight of him, tousled hair and all, made my heart flutter in a way I hadn't expected. "I figured you deserved a proper wake-up call."

"Wow, you really know how to spoil a girl," I replied, sitting up and accepting a cup of coffee from him. The warmth seeped into my hands, grounding me in the moment. I took a sip, savoring the rich flavor, while Diego leaned against the headboard, watching me with a grin that made my heart skip a beat.

After a few moments of comfortable silence, he shifted, his expression turning serious. "Before I head out, I'd love to see Sophie again. If that's okay with you." The question lingered in the air, and I felt a swell of affection mixed with a tinge of nervousness.

"Of course," I replied, imagining the way Sophie's face would light up at the prospect of spending time with Diego. "How about you come over and teach her how to kick a soccer ball? I think she'd love that."

Diego's smile widened, and I could see the excitement in his eyes. "That sounds perfect. I can't wait to show her a few tricks."

I took another sip of coffee, feeling warmth spread through me—not just from the drink, but from the thought of Diego stepping into our world and connecting with my daughter. It felt like a step forward, a piece of something I hadn't allowed myself to hope for.

Something about the sincerity of his tone last night made me hold onto every single word that left his lips, and I felt comfortable letting him see Sophie again. After all, she had been asking for him for so long.

"Let's make it happen, then," I said, a sense of determination settling within me.

As I finished my coffee, a wave of energy coursed through me. I tossed the covers aside and swung my legs over the side of the bed, feeling the cool floor beneath my feet.

"Alright, let me freshen up a bit before we leave."

Diego nodded, his eyes still dancing with warmth. "Sounds like a plan. I'll be on my best behavior."

I chuckled, shaking my head at his mock seriousness. "You? Best behavior? I'll believe it when I see it."

He raised an eyebrow playfully. "You'll see. I promise to be the perfect guest for your daughter."

I walked to the bathroom to freshen up. As I brushed my teeth, I caught my reflection in the mirror—slightly disheveled, but there was a glow about me I hadn't noticed in a while. Diego had a way of pulling me out of my shell, and I could feel the excitement bubbling within me as I thought about the day ahead.

Before heading out, I grabbed my phone and dialed my mom's number to check in on Sophie. She picked up after a couple of rings.

"Hi, Mom! Just wanted to see how things are going with Sophie. Everything okay?" I asked, trying to keep my voice casual, even though I could already imagine Sophie running around and filling the house with her endless energy.

"Oh, she's been an angel," Mom replied, her voice warm. "She's actually drawing right now. I think she's making a masterpiece for you."

I smiled, picturing Sophie's serious little face as she worked on her art. "That sounds just like her. Also, I wanted to let you know that Diego and I will be heading over soon to spend some time with her. We'll all have a little hangout together if that's okay with you."

"Of course! It'll be nice to meet him properly," she said, a hint of curiosity in her tone. "I'll let Sophie know you're on your way."

"Thanks, Mom. I'll see you soon." Ending the call, I slipped on my shoes and called out, "Ready to roll?"

"Always," Diego replied, stepping into the living area with casual confidence. He had changed into a fitted T-shirt and shorts, the perfect attire for kicking a soccer ball around with a six-year-old. "You look amazing, by the way."

"Thanks," I replied, trying to downplay the compliment, though warmth crept into my cheeks nonetheless. "Let me just grab my things, and we can head out."

As I gathered my purse and keys, Diego's gaze lingered on me, an expression I couldn't quite place—a mix of admiration and something deeper that made my heart race.

"I know things are complicated with our schedules, just as I know, but I want you to know that I'm here for you and Sophie," he said after a brief silence. "I don't want that to be just a thing I say … I want you to know that I mean it."

"I appreciate that," I said, feeling a sense of reassurance in his words. "I want this to work, Diego, but it's all new territory for me. I don't want to rush anything."

He nodded, understanding etched across his features. "Just take it one step at a time. I'm not going anywhere."

I managed a smile, feeling the weight of my apprehensions lift just a bit. We were on this journey together, and with each passing moment, I felt more hopeful about what the future could hold.

With one last glance in the mirror, I took a deep breath and opened the door. "Let's go have some fun," I said, stepping into the sunlight.

The drive to my parents place was filled with easy conversation and laughter. We shared stories about our childhoods, Diego was born in Argentina, his mother left his dad and brought him to Miami when he was just five, he was raised by a single mom and she bought him his first soccer ball which fueled his love for the game. I went on about my upbringing in Texas and all the summers my dad spent teaching me how to swim in the pool, my art project that won me a trip to the Houston Rodeo which landed me an honorable pic in the local newspaper. It felt so natural, so effortless, and I could sense the connection between us deepening.

When we arrived, my mom opened the door with Sophie at her side. Sophie's face lit up with excitement as soon as she saw me.

"Mommy!" she exclaimed, running toward me.

"Hey, sweetheart! Look who's here!" I gestured to Diego, who smiled warmly at my mom as she watched the scene unfold with quiet curiosity.

"Diego, yay!" she shouted, then dashed over and hugged Diego's legs, her small arms wrapping around him in a way that made my heart swell.

Diego bent down to Sophie's level and gave her an affectionate grin. "Hey there, superstar! Are you ready to learn some soccer skills?"

"Yes!" she squealed, clapping her hands. "Can you teach me how to kick the ball super far?"

Behind her, Mom stepped in carrying Sophie's overnight bag. "Well, look who's glowing," she said with a teasing smile.

I laughed, shaking my head. "Don't start."

Diego stepped forward. "It's good to see you again, Mrs. James."

"Charlotte," she corrected warmly, giving him a quick hug.

Her gaze lingered on me, then shifted back to him. "You've made my daughter very happy," she said softly. "I can tell. It's been a long time since I've seen her smile like that."

Diego's expression gentled. "I care about her and Sophie more than I can explain. That's all I ever want to do."

My mom nodded. "That's all a mother needs to hear. I know it's not easy with distance and schedules, but something tells me you two are going to make it through whatever comes."

He smiled, emotion flickering in his eyes. "I hope so."

She patted his arm. "Hope is a good start. Effort is the rest."

Sophie tugged Diego toward the small patch of grass in their backyard. "Come on! Let's play!" He followed, laughing, as he chased after her as she shrieked with joy. I stood by the door, watching them, with my mom's words still echoing in my head. *He's a good one, Amelia.*

She was right.

As the sun poured through the window, Diego scooped Sophie up, spinning her until she laughed uncontrollably.

But as I took in the laughter and joy surrounding us, a flutter of uncertainty gripped my heart. What if this was just a fleeting moment? What if I let myself fall deeper, only to find out he wasn't the one? That wouldn't affect only me, but my child as well. The thought sent a chill through me, and I couldn't shake the feeling that with every smile and shared glance, I was inching closer to something beautiful—and potentially terrifying.

Sixteen
Amelia

The night had finally settled down. Sophie was fast asleep, curled up with her favorite blanket, her soft breathing drifting from down the hall. Now it was just me and Diego, sitting together on the couch in the quiet, dimly lit living room.

The house felt wrapped in stillness, the kind that comes after a day full of noise and joy. The faint whir of the dishwasher was the only sound, and the soft amber light from the lamp painted everything in gold. The air still smelled faintly of popcorn and sugar from the brownies we had baked earlier. I sank deeper into the couch, letting the calm settle into me, a peace that felt new and rare.

Diego leaned back beside me, still holding my hand, his thumb tracing small, soothing circles across my skin. He hadn't said much since my mom left, but he didn't need to. The quiet between us didn't feel awkward. It felt like its own kind of conversation.

I turned my head to look at him, catching the way the light shimmered in his eyes. There was something softer about him here, away from the field, away from the noise of his world. He looked at home, stretched out on my couch, a little tired but completely at ease. It hit me how easily he blended into this version of my life, into these late-night corners that usually belonged only to me.

He studied me for a moment, as if deciding where to begin.

"I was thinking about my schedule," he said finally. "I've got a few big games coming up. Miami's the first, then a couple in L.A. and New York. It'd mean a lot to me if you and Sophie could come out to one."

For a second, I didn't answer. His offer hung in the air, sweet and heavy. My mind started spinning before my heart could catch up. Work deadlines, school, and schedules were all the things that kept my life in its careful rhythm. But then I looked up and saw the hope in his expression, that boyish mix of pride and vulnerability.

"Miami again, huh?" I smiled, my voice coming out softer than I meant. "Sophie would love that." The thought of warm air, ocean breeze, and seeing him play again flickered through my mind. Then reality pressed in. "But it's kind of a crazy time with work," I added, my fingers tightening around his. "I have an important project coming up."

He didn't let go. "I know," he said, eyes searching mine. "But maybe this is the perfect time to make it happen. I know it would mean a lot to me to have you both there. It's a home opener. It feels like the right moment for you to see me in my world … after I've seen you in yours."

His words found a place somewhere deep inside me, the part that always tried to stay grounded and resisted wanting too much. *His world.* I pictured it instantly: the crowd, the floodlights, and the stadium's pulse. Him out there, in motion, alive in a way that was both electric and unreachable. The thought of standing there, watching him from the stands, sent a small rush through me.

"I know. I want to be there too. But it's hard to step away right now with everything going on here." I traced the back of his hand absentmindedly. "Still, maybe I can make it work."

Diego's face lit up. That smile that always seemed to disarm me, no matter how much I tried to stay composed. He leaned in a little, voice dipping lower. "I'm serious. I want you there. I want you and Sophie to come out. And if it would make things easier, I'll pay for the flights and accommodations. Anything you need. I'll make sure everything's taken care of so the trip is as pleasant as possible for you both. And hey, if your girls want to come too, I'll get tickets for them, too. I want you all to be there. I want you there, in the stands, cheering for me."

The way he said it, not casual or performative, but like he *meant* it, undid me a little. It wasn't about money or convenience. It was about belonging and wanting me there enough to make sure I had no reason not to be.

I laughed softly, trying to mask the sudden warmth in my chest. "Alright," I said, meeting his gaze. "I still need to double-check everything with work, but I think it would be great. It'll be a lot of fun, and I know Sophie will love it. And it's so sweet of you to offer for the girls to come too."

Diego's grip tightened, a smile playing on his lips. "I just want you there. I want you to be part of it all. I'll take care of everything. Just think of it as a mini vacation. A chance to get away from the stress, enjoy some time together, and see me in action."

I smiled, my heart swelling with that familiar mix of excitement and fear. I'd spent so much of my life being careful, staying in control, and keeping my emotions in neat, safe boxes. But with him, that control slipped away so easily.

I took a breath that felt too full. "I'll make it work." My voice was more certain now. "As I said, I just need to sort a few things out. But I'm in."

Diego smiled as he brushed his thumb across my wrist again, his touch lingering just long enough to make my chest tighten.

"Miami, here we come," he murmured, his tone low and teasing.

For the first time in a long time, I didn't overthink what could go wrong. I just let myself imagine what could go *right*.

Seventeen
Amelia

The stadium thrummed with energy, the air thick with excitement and the promise of a new season. Miami's night pressed warm against my skin even inside the concourse, where sea-salt air seemed to follow the crowd in waves. Outside, palm fronds rattled against the breeze; inside, turquoise and coral banners rippled from the rafters, the colors of Miami Wave FC washing the stands in light. Drums pulsed from the supporters' end. It was a heartbeat that rolled through the bowl and into my chest as Victoria, Anastasia, Sophie, and I walked through the gates.

"This is amazing!" Victoria breathed, eyes wide as she took in the mosaic of jerseys, flags, and the ribbon boards chasing each other around the upper deck. "I've never been to an opening game before."

Anastasia practically vibrated beside her, turning a slow circle like she wanted to memorize everything: the mural behind the goal, the animated crest flaring on the giant screens, and the warm glow of field lights on the trimmed grass. Sophie tilted her face up at the Jumbotron, mouth parted, pointing whenever the cameras panned to players jogging in warm-ups.

We had VIP passes. Diego made sure of it. Our seats were just a few rows off the touchline, close enough to hear the studs scrape the turf and the coaches' shouts carry on the wind. The thrill of it all zipped through me. This was Diego's world, and tonight I wasn't watching it through a phone; I was in it.

I spotted him as soon as we came down the steps, his broad shoulders, easy stride, the turquoise training top hugging the lines of him as he checked a pass and spun into a one-two. He was so at home out there, the noise melting around him until it looked like he and the ball moved to a rhythm all their own. My heart tipped, pride rushing in fast and bright.

"Look, Amelia!" Victoria shot to her feet and waved. "There's Taije!" By the near sideline, Taije laughed with a couple of teammates before glancing up our way. He clocked Victoria instantly. His grin went sun-bright; he lifted a hand and waved back.

"I totally forgot about your Vegas love story," I teased, nudging her. "You two were a rom-com waiting to happen. What went wrong? Were the cocktails casting spells?"

She smirked, eyes flicking back to the field. "It was absolutely the cocktails. We're better as friends." She paused, then said, softer, "But I'm not mad about the view."

The announcer's voice rolled over us as the starting XI flashed across the boards. The supporters' section surged to its feet, scarves up, a wall of coral and turquoise swaying to the chant. I pulled Sophie close as she held up the little sign Diego had given her at the hotel: *GO DIEGO!* in bubble letters, glittered at the corners where she and Victoria had gotten a little too enthusiastic.

"I'm so excited to see him play," she whispered without looking away from the field.

"I know, baby." I kissed the top of her head. "It's going to be so much fun."

The whistle floated through the noise, and the game opened like a breath held too long. Miami pressed high, pinning the visitors in, and the patterns started to show, overlaps down the right, a quick switch to pull the back line across, Diego dropping into the half-space to collect and turn. I didn't know all the terminology, but I knew what I felt watching him: electricity and confidence. A kind of grace that only made sense on grass.

"Watch him pull the center back," Anastasia murmured, leaning in as if she'd been born in a press box. "He drifts, then suddenly, boom, space."

I arched my brow, looking at her. "Since when are you *this* familiar with soccer?"

Anastasia shrugged with a mischievous smirk. On cue, Diego let the ball run across his body, slipped a no-look pass into the channel for the winger's run, and accelerated to the box. The cross skimmed through the six and skidded out for a corner. The stadium rose to its toes.

Turquoise shirts bunched and scattered like marbles. The delivery arced toward the near post; Diego cut late across his marker, snapped his header down, and it was parried. A groan rippled; the rebound was hacked clear.

The visitors clawed back with a counter, forcing a save that made my stomach lurch before relief crashed over me. It was breathless, end-to-end, and I felt strangely steady in all the motion, because every time the ball found Diego, the game seemed to slow just enough for him to choose the next note.

Midway through the second half, with the score level and the noise swelling, it happened. Miami recycled possession, patient but hungry. The holding midfielder fizzed a pass into Diego between the lines. He let it ride, turned on his back foot, and split the defense with a slide-rule ball to the winger. The stadium leaned with the run. A first-time cutback knifed through the box and found him again, Diego ghosting to the penalty spot, defender on his shoulder. He shaped like he'd hit it across the keeper and then opened his hips and tucked it inside the near post instead.

The net snapped. Sound detonated.

I was on my feet before I knew it, shouting with everyone else, and Sophie bounced like a spring and clapped so hard the sign shook in her hands. Victoria and Anastasia screamed in my ear, and I laughed, breathless and dizzy. Diego turned toward our section in the chaos, found us, *found me*—and lifted an arm, that grin like sunlight after rain. Pride surged through me so fast it almost hurt.

The rest blurred into whistles and chants and a countdown, the fans shouted in unison. When the final whistle blew, it felt like the entire city exhaled at once. Miami Wave FC opened the season with a win, and Diego's name was on the board.

As we soaked in the energy of the crowd leaving the stadium, my phone buzzed. It was a text from Diego. I didn't even know when he had managed to grab his phone to text me.

Diego:

Dinner for all of you tonight, bring my Sophie too. Celebrating properly. I'll send a driver to the hotel in an hour.

I read it to the girls. Victoria's eyebrows climbed.

"Oh, dinner with the star." She flicked a glance toward the field. "Think Taije can be persuaded to make an appearance? For old times' sake."

Anastasia snorted. "You mean for your ego."

Victoria's smile gave her away. "Tomato, tomato."

Sophie tugged my hand. "Are we going to dinner with Diego, Mommy?"

"Yes, sweetheart." I hugged her close. "We're celebrating."

The restaurant Diego chose glowed warm and low-lit, the kind of place where the server set down bread you didn't order, and you thanked them like it was sacred. Woven cane pendants cast soft halos on the tables, and terracotta and tropical leaves softened the space into something intimate and alive. Diego waited by the host stand, freshly showered, his hair still damp at the ends. When he saw us, his face brightened, open and unguarded in a way that made the night tilt.

"Hey, there's my favorite cheer squad," he said, sweeping Sophie into a hug that made her squeal. Then he folded me into his arms with a warm, lingering press that sent my pulse flipping. "Thanks for being here," he added, looking from me to my friends. "You made my evening."

Sophie tipped her chin up, solemn and proud. "I told Mommy I wanted to see you play, and you scored."

Diego crouched to her eye level. "Then I'm taking you to every game." He winked. Sophie's smile lit the room.

We slid into a corner banquette. Conversations lapped like easy waves. Sophie peppered Diego with questions. *"How fast can you run? Do you get nervous? What do you eat before games?"* He answered each one with patience and stories that made her gasp and giggle. Taije arrived a few minutes later, all charm and dimples, and Victoria gave him a casual little wave that fooled no one.

"You remember Vegas?" she asked, airy as a feather.

Taije chuckled as he took the seat across from her. "Hard to forget a city that never sleeps and a girl who kept me laughing even when she shouldn't have."

"Friends who cheer each other on," she said, smoothing her napkin like she wasn't blushing.

"Always," he said, eyes warm.

I smiled, not missing the way she looked at him before she turning her attention to the rest of the table.

Dinner slid from appetizers to entrées without anyone noticing the time. I found myself relaxing in a way I hadn't in months, like some tight knot inside me had finally loosened. Diego didn't perform; he made space. For Sophie's questions. For Victoria's dry one-liners. For Anastasia's stories. For me.

When the girls slipped off to the restroom together, Sophie between them, her tiny hand tucked into each of theirs, the table suddenly felt quieter and private. Diego's attention shifted fully to me.

"Having you here with Sophie is more special than I can say." His voice softened, the confidence he wore on the field giving way to something more careful.

"Seeing you in your element, hearing the crowd say your name, and watching Sophie light up made tonight feel like a piece of your life I could actually hold."

He reached across the table and threaded our fingers together, his thumb brushing a slow line over my knuckles. "You bring something I didn't know I was missing," he said, eyes steady on mine. "When I looked up after the goal and saw you," He shook his head with a small, helpless smile. "It settled me."

The truth of it pressed warm against my ribs. I wanted to believe this could be as simple as it felt, and I wanted it enough that I could hear my own caution trying to keep up. Houston. Work. Sophie's rhythm. The distance. But with his hand around mine, the noise dimmed. My walls didn't crash; they eased, like a door left slightly ajar.

The girls returned, Victoria clocking our linked hands with a grin she tried and failed to hide. "So," she sang under her breath as she slid in, "when's our next game trip? Strictly for morale."

"We'll see," I laughed, and Diego's fingers gave mine a gentle squeeze.

"No pressure," he said, low enough for only me to hear. "But anytime you're here, I'm here."

By dessert, Sophie was fighting yawns hard enough to topple a statue. Anastasia caught my eye, then nudged Victoria.

"I think someone's ready for a cartoon marathon," Victoria announced lightly. "Robes, room service, and a hotly contested debate between a few of our favorite cartoons?"

Sophie perked up just enough to whisper, "Both," which sealed the plan.

"Perfect," I said, warmth sliding through me at how easily my friends made space for what they knew I needed—even before I could ask.

Taije lingered near Victoria as we stood. "After you tuck in Princess," he murmured, "maybe we can find a quiet corner for one drink. For old times' sake."

The teasing glint in his eye earned him a playful eye roll and an unbothered, "We'll see," which meant yes.

Anastasia gathered Sophie with a wink for me. "We've got her. You go enjoy your night."

I pressed a kiss to Sophie's hair, thanked them, and watched the three of them disappear into the hum of the restaurant. When I turned back, Diego was already there, close enough that the rest of the room went gently out of focus.

"Looks like it's just us," he said, voice dipped and quiet, his thumb tracing a slow circle over the back of my hand. "Let's head outside."

The night air felt charged as we stepped out, cars sliding by in soft streams of light, the ocean somewhere nearby breathing in and out. Both of us could only focus on one thing, though.

We barely made it inside his place before the distance folded. Diego's hands found my waist, my back, and my jaw, like he had been holding himself still for hours and finally let the current take him. He paused with the gentlest check, and I nodded before he even asked. That small mercy, that pause tipped something deep in me.

He kissed me like he had been replaying the moment since the goal, slow at first, then deeper, heat unspooling between us. I rose onto my toes; he gathered me closer. The city glowed through the windows in soft neon and moonlight, washing the room in a quiet shimmer. I could feel the echo of the stadium in his pulse, the steadiness of it settling against mine.

"My God, how I've missed you," he whispered against my mouth, and the words landed everywhere at once.

We moved without hurry and without space, laughter spilled between kisses, a soft gasp when his hands found the small of my back, the press of my fingers at his collar as if I could memorize him by touch. I wanted to memorize him everywhere, all at once, and he wanted to do the same in return.

He lifted me; I didn't let go. Somewhere along the way, we had found our way to connect, and he slid himself deep into me—right where he belonged. I whimpered in pleasure, my eyes rolling back into my skull. Passion edged everything brighter, every kiss, every exhale, every yes, until the moment tipped over and we slipped with it, heat and light and the softest break in the middle of it all.

"Just like that," I pleaded, and he continued to move with the same pace, worshipping my body with his. His hot mouth was everywhere, all over my jaw, my chest, my breasts, my neck. Neither of us could get enough. Both of us wishing the moment to last forever.

Outside, the city breathed. Inside, we found our own rhythm, urgent and sure, until the night blurred at the edges and the rest of it didn't matter anymore. Together, we reached our peaks, with his shaft buried so deep inside me that I never wanted it to leave.

Later, quiet and sated beneath the hush of the room, the lights still pooling in strips across the floor, he traced an absentminded line along my wrist. I listened to his breathing and the faraway sigh of the ocean and the way my body had finally, finally settled.

Eighteen
Amelia

I woke to the sound of soft Miami waves and the golden light streaming through the bedroom curtains. Diego's arm was draped over me, his breathing slow and even. For a moment, I let myself just be. No work deadlines, no Sophie to tend to, and no distance between us.

Diego stirred, his dark eyes meeting mine as a lazy grin spread across his face. "*Buenos días*," he murmured, his voice husky with sleep.

"Good morning," I replied, unable to suppress a small smile of my own.

He stretched, pulling me closer. "Last night was incredible. I could not have wished for a better way to spend it."

I felt the sincerity in his words, the warmth of his gratitude. "We loved being there. Sophie could not stop talking about your goal."

Diego chuckled, the sound rumbling through his chest. "She's a good luck charm. You both are." He sat up slightly, resting on one elbow as he looked at me. "I know your schedule is crazy, but it would mean so much if you could make it to more games. Home or away, whatever works. I want you there. I want us to make this a regular thing. And of course, in return, I'll visit whenever I can, Mostly out of season."

His words hung in the air, full of hope but also expectation. I hesitated, choosing my next words carefully. "Diego, I loved being there last night. Truly. But you know my work is demanding, and I can't just—"

"Drop everything," he finished for me, his tone gentle but firm. "I get it. I do. But this is important to me. You're important to me. And I'm trying to build something here, not just with my career but with us."

I sighed, running a hand through my hair. "It's not that I don't want to be there. It's just that this was a lot to put together. Lisa practically moved mountains to make my schedule work for this trip, and Sophie's school does not exactly encourage spontaneous absences. It's not as easy as it looks."

Diego frowned, his playful expression fading. "I'm not asking for easy. I'm asking for effort. The same effort I'm putting in."

His words stung, though I knew he did not mean them harshly. Still, I found myself sitting up and shaking my head. "You think I'm not making an effort?"

"I think you're scared to," he said, his voice steady but quiet. "You've got one foot in and one foot out. And I get it—you're protecting yourself. But if this is going to work, we both need to be all in. You need to know I won't hurt you. And we need to figure out a way to see each other despite all the obstacles we may face ..."

I turned to face him. "I'm doing the best I can. Between work, Sophie, and everything else, I don't have the same kind of freedom you do. And honestly, if that's what you're looking for, I don't know if I'll ever be able to give you that."

The room fell silent, the weight of my words settling between us. Diego ran a hand over his face and exhaled deeply. "I'm not asking for perfection. Just let's both try to meet each other halfway. That's what you wanted in the first place, isn't it?"

His vulnerability hit me harder than I expected. He wasn't just talking about games or schedules. He was talking about us—about whether I was truly ready to let him into my life, or if I was still holding back out of fear. I paused for a moment to think about it. I wanted this, but a part of me was still terrified I'd get hurt.

"I'm not trying to make this harder than it already is," I said softly, reaching for his hand. "I care about you. And I want this to work. But it's going to take time to figure out how on both our sides. I hope you can understand that … and make it happen with me."

Diego nodded slowly, his expression a mixture of understanding and frustration. "Time, I can work with. But I need to know you're in this with me and that you're not looking for an out every time things get complicated." He reached for my cheek, stroking it gently, and I felt that familiar twist in my stomach that I so desperately tried to ignore.

I didn't have an answer for him, not one that would fix everything. All I could do was hold his hand and hope it was enough for now.

The sharp buzz of my phone broke through the quiet like a lifeline. I reached for it instinctively, relieved by the interruption.

"Hello?" I answered, my voice steady, though my thoughts were tangled.

"Hey, Amelia," came Anastasia's voice on the other end. "Sorry to call so early, but someone insisted on talking to you."

"Mommy?" Sophie's excited voice chimed in, making my shoulders relax instantly.

"Hi, sweetheart!" I said, a smile tugging at my lips. "How's it going?"

"Good! We just had breakfast. Auntie Victoria let me have pancakes with chocolate syrup!" she exclaimed.

I laughed softly. "Lucky you. Did you have fun last night with the girls?"

"It was the best! But when are you coming back?" Her voice softened, and I could almost see her little frown.

"We'll head back soon," I promised. "Diego and I will come by to pick you up before we go to the airport."

Diego had been sitting quietly on the edge of the bed, leaning forward with his elbows on his knees as he listened. At the mention of his name, he straightened. "I'll grab my things and get us ready," he said, standing.

"Okay, we'll see you soon," I said to Sophie before hanging up.

I looked at Diego as he started gathering his jacket and keys. "You don't have to take me, you know. We can grab a cab."

"I want to," he replied firmly. "I'd like to say goodbye to Sophie anyway."

I hesitated, then nodded. "Okay."

Nineteen

Diego

I grabbed my jacket and keys without another word, but inside, I was still carrying the weight of the conversation Amelia and I had just had. She didn't say she was all in, but she didn't walk away either. And that was enough for now. It was strange that we found ourselves in this situation, with both of us trying to step forward when the other retreated, just slightly.

She stood by the bed collecting her things, avoiding my eyes in that careful way she did when her thoughts were moving too fast. I knew she needed space to settle her feelings, and the last thing I wanted was to push harder than I already had.

"I mean it. I'll take you back to the hotel," I said again, this time quieter.

She gave a small nod, the kind that told me she wasn't ready to argue but wasn't ready to say more either. We left the condo together, stepping into the elevator. The ride down was quiet, but not from tension, just two people holding onto their own thoughts, replaying everything that had been said.

I should've felt frustrated. But instead, I felt hopeful. She didn't shut down or pull away. She wanted time, and I could give her that.

When we reached the parking garage, she slipped into the passenger seat while I loaded her overnight bag. The moment I shut the trunk; I let myself breathe. This weekend had been a lot for both of us, but there was something here that neither of us wanted to give up on.

On the short drive back, Amelia watched the palm trees pass outside her window, her fingertips tapping lightly against her thigh. She wasn't distant—just somewhere in her own mind, sorting through what came next. I didn't force conversation.

When we pulled up to the hotel, she turned to me. "I'm going to run upstairs and finish packing. I'll be quick."

"I'll wait," I said.

She hesitated like she wanted to thank me, but didn't know how to form the words without reopening the conversation we had left hanging. Instead, she gave me a small, tired smile and headed inside. As she disappeared through the glass doors, I leaned back in the driver's seat, letting the quiet settle around me.

The truth was simple: I didn't want to take her to the airport. I didn't want this weekend to end. I wanted more time, more mornings, more moments, and more of the softness I saw in her when she let her guard down. But wanting something and rushing it weren't the same thing. She wasn't running from me—she was trying to figure out how to let herself stay. And that mattered.

Ten minutes later, my phone buzzed.

Amelia:

We're heading down.

I stepped out of the car just as Sophie burst through the hotel doors, her little backpack dangling off one shoulder. "Diego!" she shouted, running straight toward me.

I caught her mid-jump. There was something about her excitement—pure, bright, and uncomplicated—that made everything else feel lighter. Plus, Mr. Buttons was right there with her for moral support.

"Ready to go?" I asked.

She shook her head immediately. "No! I want to stay. This weekend was the best!"

Amelia walked up behind her, her hair pulled back, her suitcase rolling smoothly behind her. Anastasia and Victoria followed, finishing their coffees and giving me that quiet, watchful look—protective, but warm.

"Let me get that," I said, taking Amelia's suitcase before she could lift it.

She didn't fight me on it. "Thanks." Once I was done with her suitcase, I did the same for the girls, too, helping them load everything up.

Once everything was loaded, Sophie fidgeted with her backpack straps, looking up at me. "Can we do something fun before we go home?"

I glanced at Amelia. She shrugged, a tiny smile appearing. "She's been asking all morning."

"Actually …" I said, closing the trunk, "I have an idea."

I drove them toward the quiet beach near the inlet, a place I always went when I needed clarity, or calm, or a reminder of home. When the shoreline came into view, Sophie practically vibrated.

"The *beach*?" she squealed.

Amelia laughed under her breath, shaking her head as she looked at me. "I don't know who's more excited, you or her."

The sun was warm but not harsh, the waves pushing gently against the sand. Sophie sprinted straight toward the waterline, shoes flying, arms outstretched like a little airplane. I followed her, keeping a careful eye on the incoming tide, but she was too busy searching for seashells to notice anything else.

"This one looks like a heart!" she shouted, holding up a small white shell.

I knelt beside her. "That's a good one. Really good."

She pressed it into my hand. "It's for you. So, you remember Miami with us."

I swallowed. The kid had no idea how deeply that hit. "I won't forget this, Soph."

Behind us, Amelia stood with her arms folded, watching us with a softness she didn't try to hide. I walked back toward her, brushing sand off my palms.

"She's going to make a whole sandcastle in her suitcase," I teased lightly, and Amelia laughed. It loosened something in my chest. The girls wandered down the shoreline, giving us a moment alone. Amelia stepped closer, the wind pulling a strand of hair across her cheek. I reached out gently to tuck it behind her ear. She didn't pull away.

"Thank you for bringing us here," she said. "This was … really nice."

I shrugged lightly, but inside something tightened. "You deserve a calm end to the weekend."

She held my gaze a second longer than she meant to, and I felt all the things neither of us was ready to say.

Eventually, Amelia checked the time. "We should head out," she said reluctantly. I nodded in agreement.

The drive to the airport was quieter again—just the natural lull of people who didn't want a good thing to end. When I pulled up to the departure lane, Sophie leaned over the console to hug me.

"You'll visit, right?" she asked.

"Yes," I said immediately. "Soon."

Anastasia and Victoria said their goodbyes, and then it was just Amelia. She stepped closer, her hand brushing my forearm.

"Thank you," she murmured.

"For what?"

"For this morning. For driving us. For … being you." She exhaled. "And for being so patient."

I cupped her jaw gently. No pushing. No forcing. Just a quiet promise in the touch. "Text me when you land," I said.

She nodded, her eyes softer than they had been all morning. Then she grabbed Sophie's hand, and walked toward the sliding doors. Halfway there, she turned back just for a second. And that second was enough to remind me whatever this was, whatever we were building, I was in it. For real.

Twenty
Amelia

Back in Houston, the sound of Sophie's laughter drifted through the house, mingling with the faint hum of the washing machine and the smell of freshly brewed coffee. I stood in the kitchen, staring at my laptop screen, a half-written email glaring back at me. It was Monday morning, and I was already behind. The weekend felt like a dream: the stadium lights washing over him, the crowd roaring every time he touched the ball, and the way his gaze kept finding me in the stands like I was the only person he could see. For those moments, everything felt suspended. But now, reality was settling in, like it usually did once I came back to Houston.

"Mommy, can I wear my Diego jersey to school?" Sophie called out from the living room, her little feet pattering against the floor.

I smiled despite myself, shutting the laptop and turning toward her. She stood there, holding the bright green jersey as if it were a treasure. Her cheeks were still flushed with excitement from the weekend, her eyes sparkling in a way that reminded me of Diego's.

"Not today, sweetheart," I said gently, kneeling to her level. "You've got to wear your uniform, but maybe after school, okay?"

She pouted for a moment before nodding. "Okay. Can we call him later? I want to tell him about the dinosaur book Auntie Victoria got me!"

"We'll see," I said, brushing a strand of hair from her face. "Diego's busy with practice this week."

The mention of his name sent a pang through my chest. I hadn't texted him since we landed in Houston last night. It wasn't that I didn't want to; it was that I didn't know what to say. The weekend had been wonderful, but it had also stirred up feelings I wasn't ready to face. It was like he was already planning a future I wasn't sure I could give him. Not because I didn't want to, but because I wasn't sure whether I could ever fully let go of control like he wanted me to. And then there was the conversation about effort, about commitment. His words replayed in my mind like a broken record: "You've got one foot in and one foot out, Amelia."

I couldn't stop replaying my conversation with Diego in my head. He'd been honest, maybe too honest about what he wanted from me, and I couldn't blame him for that. But the moment he said he wanted me at his games to show my support, I froze. It wasn't that I didn't want to be there. Of course, I did. But could I realistically juggle it all—Sophie, work, and him, without losing myself in the process? And, more importantly, could I dare to choose someone so unconditionally?

"Mommy?" Sophie's voice broke through my thoughts. "Are you okay?"

I blinked, forcing a smile. "I'm fine, baby. Just thinking about work."

She didn't look convinced, but she nodded anyway, skipping off to finish her breakfast. I watched her go, my heart aching with the knowledge that she deserved so much more than my half-hearted reassurances.

Once she was settled at the table, I grabbed my phone and stared at the screen. Diego's name sat at the top of my messages, unanswered. My fingers hovered over the keyboard before I finally typed out a simple text.

Me:

Thanks again for the weekend. I'm just taking care of Sophie and making sure everything runs smoothly.

I hit send before I could overthink it, setting the phone face down on the counter. It buzzed almost immediately, and my stomach twisted as I flipped it over.

Diego:

Glad to hear. I hope all is going well. I miss you already.

Four words. So simple, yet they carried the weight of everything I was trying to avoid. I stared at the screen, my thumb hovering over the keyboard, but before I could respond, my work phone buzzed on the counter, snapping me back to reality.

Mr. Thompson.

I groaned, swiping to answer. "Hi, Mr. Thompson."

"Morning, Amelia," he said briskly. "Did you have a good weekend?"

"Yes, it was nice," I replied, trying to keep my tone professional.

"Good, because we've got a packed week ahead. I need your pitch for the new Lumera Beauty campaign by tomorrow. And I want to see your expanded notes on the brand strategy by the end of the day."

My stomach tightened. Lumera Beauty was one of our biggest clients this quarter, an eco-luxe skincare line launching their new clean-beauty collection. Their founder, Isabel Reyes, was brilliant but demanding, and she expected perfection from me.

"Got it," I said, scribbling down his demands on a sticky note.

"This Glow Renewal launch is massive for them. I want the 'Refresh. Renew. Reclaim.' messaging integrated everywhere, landing copy, social drafts, influencer scripts. And don't forget the expanded rollout for the 30-Day Glow Challenge. They want more lifestyle angles and a stronger community hook. They're expecting a full proposal."

"I'll get it together," I told him. "Don't you worry."

"Good. I need you to be fully present this week. Can I count on you?"

I glanced at Sophie, still humming over her cereal. "Of course. You can count on me."

When the call ended, I took a slow breath. Being the marketing director at Elite Source meant every major account was stacked on me, along with every strategy and deadline. Especially launches like Lumera's that demanded creativity, innovation, and a hundred moving pieces.

I picked up my coffee, opened my laptop again, and stared at my inbox. Lumera assets, campaign notes, mood boards, a reminder about the brand's pop-up at Discovery Green. Influencer requests. A stack of tasks so tall I could barely see over it. Still, I'd tackle it one by one, like I always did.

First, I took Sophie to school, kissed her cheek, and watched her run toward the entrance with her backpack bouncing behind her. Then I finally had a moment alone to breathe as I drove toward the office.

On the way, I called Lisa.

"Morning, Amelia!" Lisa chirped.

"Morning, Lisa. Can you schedule a meeting for this afternoon around three? Thompson dumped a ton of Lumera updates on me. I want everyone aligned before we start delegating."

"Got it," she said, typing quickly. "I'll check availability and send invites."

"And pull every outstanding item related to Lumera. I need a clean view of what's left."

"Absolutely."

"Thanks, Lisa. See you soon."

Work was predictable and structured. It was a place where I could control the outcome if I worked hard enough. Unlike everything else in my life.

By the time I reached the office, the building gleamed with its usual intimidating calm. The conference room was already buzzing when I walked in, laptop under my arm.

"Morning, everyone," I said, taking my seat. "We've got a lot to cover."

I connected my screen and pulled up the Lumera Beauty campaign deck. Their aesthetic filled the room—soft sage, sand beige, and luminous gold accents. Clean. Fresh. Elevated.

"Okay," I began. "Here's where we stand with the Glow Renewal launch. This is all about positioning Lumera as elevated but accessible. Three pillars: sustainability, sensorial experience, and skin confidence."

I clicked on the slide showing their hero product.

"The Glow Renewal Serum is the centerpiece. Our visuals should emphasize real results, visible texture, natural dewiness, and raw skin. No smoothing filters. No fake perfection." Nods filled the room. "We're also building a full-funnel rollout: email journeys, ASMR-style short-form videos, a hero shoot featuring unretouched models, and influencer storytelling through the 30-Day Glow Challenge." I switched slides again. "For the challenge, we're prioritizing creators who feel authentic. Wellness creators, Latina micro influencers, clean-girl aesthetic content creators. There will be weekly check-ins, GRWM routines, and honest progress videos."

Lisa leaned in. "Want me to take the lead on outreach?"

"Yes. Engagement rate over follower count. Lumera wants conversions, not vanity numbers."

"And the pop-up?" someone asked.

"Yes. Discovery Green. We're pitching a refill station for their Eco Dew Drops. A sustainability activation that lets community members bring in their bottles for discounted refills."

Right then, Mr. Thompson walked into the room, clipboard in hand.

"Don't mind me," he said. "Just wanted to commend Amelia on the skincare pitch last week. Lumera's founder loved it. Keep the momentum."

"Thank you," I said.

"And I want the retargeting ads sharper," he added. "We're selling a ritual, not a product."

"I'll handle it," I assured him.

Once he left, Lisa whispered dramatically, "Translation: we're living here for a month."

I stifled a laugh. "Probably."

The meeting wrapped up, and I returned to my office, where my phone buzzed again.

Diego:

Just thinking about you. Hope your day is going well

A small smile tugged at my lips.

Me:

It's been a busy day back at work, but I miss you! Let's FaceTime when I get off work?

Diego:

Of course, baby. I look forward to it.

I slipped my phone away as Lisa leaned into the doorway.

"Deep in thought?" she asked.

"Just trying to keep my head above water."

She nodded sympathetically. "Take a walk later. You've earned it."

I smiled faintly. "Maybe."

I turned back to my computer. The Lumera campaign folder sat open, filled with subfolders; UGC scripts, campaign hashtags, brand tone rewrites, ad concepts, event decks, influencer lists, blog outlines, videos, templates, and everything else that needed to be done. It was a mountain of work, but one I was used to climbing.

But even as I dove back into deadlines, meetings, and glowing serums, Diego's face kept drifting into my mind.

Despite the pressure, the expectations, and the weight of my entire life sitting on my shoulders, I couldn't ignore the truth: part of me missed him, and I wasn't so sure I could handle the distance as well as I wanted to.

Twenty-One
Amelia

Finally, it was Friday. The week had felt like a marathon, and I was more than ready to relax. My parents had taken Sophie on a little weekend trip outdoors, and Diego was traveling to Arizona for a game. We Facetimed throughout the week, between my work and his training, but it still felt like too long to go without seeing him.

So, I did what any single mother would do when she was left all alone. I called my girlfriends over for dinner. Pasta, wine, and a *Gossip Girl* marathon. They were exactly what I needed to kick off the night and take my mind off everything else.

By the time my friends arrived, the house smelled like garlic and basil, and a pot of pasta was simmered on the stove. The wine was already opened, and everything was set for the kind of evening we all needed.

Victoria was the first to walk in, a bottle of wine in hand. "I'm so ready for this," she said, her face lighting up as she kicked off her shoes at the door.

Anastasia followed right behind, carrying a dessert that I knew would disappear in minutes. "You're really pulling out all the stops tonight, huh?"

"Only the best for my girls," I replied, trying to smile through the tension that had been gnawing at me all week. "Dinner's almost ready. You two set up, I'll bring it to the table."

We settled around the table with glasses of wine in hand, and for a moment, the conversation was light, work, the latest gossip, and life in general, but I knew it wouldn't stay that way for long. We had spent the weekend together in Miami, so they knew I had a lot on my mind, and I knew they were waiting for me to open up.

It was Victoria who finally broke the silence. "Alright, so we are all dying to know about your night with Diego in Miami? We saw how much fun Sophie had, but what about you and Diego?"

I smiled, thinking back to Sophie running into Diego's arms after his game. "Sophie had a blast. She was so excited to see him play, and Diego was great with her. They really seemed to click. It was honestly adorable."

"Girl, we know that." Anastasia leaned in, her eyes curious. "And what about you? Things still going well with him?"

I hesitated for a moment, stirring my pasta absentmindedly. I had been avoiding this part of the conversation all week, but I couldn't keep it in anymore. "We had a conversation before I left Miami," I began slowly. "About us. About where we're going. And it didn't go the way I hoped."

Anastasia and Victoria exchanged glances, and I could see both of them already sensing there was more to the story.

"What happened?" Victoria asked, her tone gentle but insistent.

I took a deep breath. "He told me that I wasn't really showing up for him. That I had one foot in, one foot out. And I think he's right. I'm not sure I'm ready to give him everything he wants. I'm not sure if I can. After Brad …"

Victoria shook her head instantly. "Don't even get me started on that man."

Anastasia's expression softened. "I know this is tough. You've been through so much with him, and I know it's hard to fully trust anyone after that. But you're letting that fear hold you back from something that could actually be really good for you."

Victoria nodded, sipping her wine. "Yeah, you've already let him into your life in big ways; he's been there with Sophie, and he's shown he wants to be there for both of you. You've already taken so many steps, even if it feels scary."

I swallowed hard, feeling a knot form in my chest. "But what if I get hurt again? What if I'm not enough for him? What if I end up in the same place I was with Brad?"

Victoria reached over, her hand gently resting on mine. "Diego isn't Brad. He's not going to hurt you the same way. You've already shown him your life, your daughter … that's a huge step for you. Don't let fear push him away before you even give him a chance."

"I know," I whispered. "But it's easier to keep things casual. To hold back. I can control that. I can protect myself that way."

Anastasia's voice was soft but firm. "You can't control everything, though. And if you keep holding back, you'll push him away. He deserves to know that you're in this with him, not just testing the waters. I know you're scared, but you're sabotaging something good because you're afraid of being vulnerable."

I felt a pang in my chest. "What if I'm just not enough for him? What if he needs more than I can give?"

"Then let *him* decide that," Victoria said. "But you can't keep shutting him out. You deserve someone who will support you and show up for you. Diego seems to want to be that person. Don't walk away from that just because you're afraid."

I was quiet for a long moment, turning their words over in my mind. I had been so afraid of being hurt again, of failing, and letting Sophie down. But deep down, I knew they were right. I couldn't keep running from the possibility of something good just for the sake of fear.

Anastasia and Victoria looked at each other, and I could see something pass between them—something mischievous and determined, the kind of energy that always meant they were about to nudge me toward a truth I'd been avoiding.

Victoria leaned back, twirling her wine glass. "Show him. Don't just *say* you're in—show him in a way he'll feel."

I frowned. "Vic, how do I even do that?"

Anastasia gave me that soft, knowing smile. "He's in Arizona right now, and you're here spiraling. What if—you don't have to commit yet—what if you flew out? Just to be with him. Not to fix anything."

My stomach flipped. "I can't just hop on a plane."

"Yes, you can," Victoria said, her voice gentler than her words. "For once, stop talking yourself out of something good for you."

I opened my mouth, the excuses already forming. "It's last-minute. Flights are expensive. I have work on Monday. And Sophie—"

Anastasia shook her head. "Your mom already has Sophie. Just let her know, she won't mind keeping her longer. She loves the extra time. I have miles. A ton of them. Let me help with the flight. It's not a big deal. I *want* to."

The sincerity in her voice cracked something inside me. She wasn't pushing me for the drama of it—she genuinely believed I deserved this.

Victoria leaned forward, elbows on the table. "You've been living in fear for so long, you don't even recognize when something real is right in front of you. Diego has been showing up for you. Let him see you're willing to show up too."

I stared at the candle between us, my heart beating too fast. "What if he doesn't want me to come?"

"He does," Victoria said without hesitation. "He asked for reassurance. He asked for presence. This is you giving him exactly what he's been brave enough to ask for."

"And you won't be alone," Anastasia added softly. "We'll help with everything. We'll help you pack and plan everything. Just let yourself try."

Their words settled over me, like a hand pressed between my shoulder blades, gently guiding me toward something I already wanted.

"I'll think about it," I whispered, though there was a softness to the words, like part of me had already said yes.

Victoria reached across the table, slid my phone off the placemat, and placed it gently in my hand.

"Text him now," she said. "Let him hear from you. Start there."

Twenty-Two
Amelia

My thumb hovered over the screen, Victoria's words echoing in my head. *Text him now.* So, I did.

Me:

> Missing you more than ever.

The message was simple and not overthought, for once. I hit send before I could take it back. The moment it was delivered, anxiety fluttered low in my stomach, but it was a softer ache than usual. I needed to ground myself, so I called my mom.

"Hey, sweetheart," she answered, warm as always.

"Hi. Just checking on Sophie."

My mom chuckled. "She's outside right now showing your father a 'magic rock' she found. It's literally just a rock. But don't tell her that."

I smiled, relief easing my chest. "Sounds like she's having a blast."

"She is," my mom said, and then paused, as if she could sense that something was wrong. "What's going on?"

I swallowed. "I booked a last-minute trip. Just overnight. I'll be back Sunday."

"Oh?" she asked, but her tone said she already knew.

"Arizona. Diego has a game. I want to surprise him."

I expected hesitation from her. It wasn't like me to do something like this. Instead, she softened. "Amelia, go. Truly. We've got Sophie. Don't worry about a thing."

My throat tightened. "Thank you. Really."

"You deserve something that makes you excited again. Don't run from it."

When I hung up, Anastasia was already holding her phone and a card.

"Alright," she said, typing like she was possessed. "Earliest flight out is 7:02 AM. Nonstop. You'll land at noon. Enough time to shower, look hot, and have a full cinematic main character montage."

Victoria was beside her, fingers flying on her phone. "I'm texting Taije, maybe he can give us the details with the hotel and help surprise Diego." A ping. Victoria grinned. "He says, and I quote, 'I live for this shit.' Team hotel is Desert Bloom. He'll make sure Diego comes down to the lobby post-game, fake that he wants to grab a bite to eat or something."

My heart kicked. *This was happening.*

By the time they shoved my packed bag into my hands, I could barely feel my limbs.

"Go," Anastasia urged. "Shave your legs, cry on the plane, whatever you need. Just go see your man."

***

Sleep didn't really happen. I woke before my alarm, showered, and slipped out into the still dark morning, nerves buzzing under my skin.

At the airport, everything felt electric. The coffee didn't touch the butterflies, and my leg bounced through the entire flight. The closer we got to Phoenix, the harder it was to breathe normally, as if the air itself were charged with him.

When the plane touched down just after noon, the desert heat rushed in through the taxi window, warm and bright and completely different from home.

The taxi pulled up to the Desert Bloom Hotel, all clean lines, soft desert tones, and understated luxury. And thanks to a very enthusiastic Taije, a room key was waiting for me at check-in. Not on the team's floor, and that was on purpose. He didn't want Diego accidentally spotting me.

My hands shook slightly when I unlocked the door. I set my bag down, exhaled, and checked my phone. Waiting for me was a message from Diego.

Diego:

About to head into pregame, but... your text earlier meant more than you know.
I miss you, too.

Diego:

Wish I could see you today. Soon, I hope.

Something warm spread through me, loosening the tight knot in my chest. He had no idea how soon. I typed back.

Me:

You've been on my mind all morning. Play your heart out today. I'll be thinking of you.

Diego:

Always better when you're thinking of me.

The reassurance settled me in a way I didn't expect.

I jumped in the shower, letting the steam calm my nerves, then blow-dried my hair until it fell in soft waves. My makeup came next. It was slow and steady, almost meditative. A simple outfit felt right: a fitted black top, jeans that hugged just right, and a touch of perfume on my wrists.

As I finished getting ready, I pulled up the team's livestream and set my phone on the dresser. Watching him on the field, so focused, fierce, and completely in his element, pulled something inside me and then melted all at once. Around 2:45 PM, Victoria's text popped up.

Victoria:

Checking in — game ends around 3ish. Taije says he'll stall Diego afterward. Just be ready around 5 at the latest. I'll let you know when to go downstairs!! OMG!!

I took a breath. Then another. This was really happening. Plus, Miami won the game.

The moment the final whistle blew, and the team rushed onto the field, I felt something warm break open inside me. I knew it would take at least an hour before they left the stadium. Enough time to calm my nerves. Or try to.

I grabbed my phone and called Sophie.

She answered immediately, her little voice bright. "Mommy!"

My heart softened. "Hi, sweetie! Are you having fun with Nana and Papa?"

She told me about the rock she found, about the marshmallows, about how Nana let her stay up "a teeny tiny bit late." Her excitement steadied me, grounding me in something familiar and safe. We talked until her voice started to get sleepy around the edges.

"Okay, baby," I said gently. "I'll see you tomorrow night, okay, have a good nap, I love you."

"Love you more! And so does Mr. Buttons!"

When the call ended, the room went quiet again, but it wasn't the same kind of nervous quiet as before. It was steadier and clearer as my phone buzzed.

Victoria:
Start heading downstairs now. Taije says they're walking out in 10. It's happening.

My breath caught. This was it. I checked the mirror one last time: soft waves, flushed cheeks, and the kind of nerves that made everything feel sharp and alive. Then I grabbed my purse and headed for the elevator, heart racing with every floor the numbers blinked through.

The lobby bar was soft lit and cool, with floor-to-ceiling windows and the desert sun pouring through. I ordered sparkling wine to hold, so my hands wouldn't shake.

Minutes later, the elevator chimed.

I didn't turn, but I heard the energy shift. There was a ripple and whispering, and then someone saying his name. Quick footsteps followed. Fans asked for photos. Autographs. Voices overlapped.

When I lifted my gaze from my glass, he was already looking.

He froze mid-sentence, mid-autograph, mid-everything, eyes locked on me from across the lobby. His whole face changed. Taije smirked behind him. Diego moved first, past the fans and the noise, straight to me.

"Amelia," he said, breathless, stunned.

"I told you," I whispered. "I hoped I'd see you soon."

He didn't hesitate. His hands cupped my face, and he kissed me. Deep, warm, and utterly undone. He lifted me effortlessly, spinning just enough that I laughed into his mouth, my hands gripping his shoulders.

"You're really here," he murmured against my cheek.

"I needed to see you."

He pressed his forehead to mine, and the whole world fell away. For a moment, it was just us, breathing in the same slow, stolen rhythm, holding onto each other like we were afraid the moment might vanish if we blinked too fast.

"Okay, okay, relax," Taije blurted out behind Diego, sounding far too pleased with himself. "I didn't plan a whole covert mission just to watch you two make out in the middle of the lobby."

Diego groaned softly but didn't step back from me. "Bro …"

"No, no, don't 'bro' me," Taije said, hands up like he was defending himself in court. "I just secured you both the hottest reservation within a ten-mile radius. Candlelight. Steak. You're welcome."

I laughed. Diego dropped his forehead to my shoulder for a half-second, shaking his head in disbelief.

"Taije," he muttered, "you're unbelievable."

"I know," Taije grinned. "It's a burden being this thoughtful." He started backing away, finger guns at the ready. "Dinner for two. Walk in whenever you want. Don't do anything I wouldn't do."

"Which is literally everything," Diego called back.

Taije winked. "Exactly."

Diego turned back to me, his hands sliding from my waist to my hips. He leaned in, brushing his thumb along my jaw, eyes completely soft. "Thank you for coming," he whispered. "I still don't believe you're here."

"I'm here," I breathed. "Right here."

His gaze traced mine, slow, tender, and hungry in a way that made my heart stumble. He was about to kiss me again.

"…Millie?" The voice cracked through the room like a glass shattering. Deep. Familiar. Unwelcome. Diego's expression shifted instantly from confusion to concern. His hand tightened slightly on my hip as he instinctively angled his body closer to mine. My stomach dropped.

No.

I turned before I could stop myself.

Brad.

He stood a few feet away, tall, composed, with a woman's hand threaded through his. A diamond ring gleamed under the soft lobby lights on her hand. She looked elegant, her gaze slipping between us with polite confusion.

Brad didn't smile. He didn't frown either. He just stared, like he was trying to place me in some distant memory that no longer mattered.

"Millie?" he said again, tone flat.

Diego shifted subtly, stepping closer. He didn't know who Brad was yet, but he sensed everything. Brad finally blinked, glancing at Diego before settling his gaze back on me, unreadable.

"Wow," he continued. "Didn't expect to see you here. Small world."

That was it. No hello. No acknowledgment of the child he had not bothered to ask about in years. *Nothing.*

The woman beside him looked between us, clearly waiting for an introduction he had no intention of giving. Brad glanced at his watch.

"We should get going," he told the woman lightly, then gave me a small nod. "Take care, Millie." He turned away before I could breathe, his hand guiding the woman toward the exit like I was nothing more than a stranger he had once sat next to on a plane.

My chest constricted, while Diego stayed exactly where he was.

"*Amelia*," he repeated, his voice barely touching the air. "Look at me."

I did. His eyes weren't confused, jealous or angry. They were steady and soft in a way that made something inside me wobble.

"I'm right here," he said quietly. My pulse was hammering. My lungs couldn't decide whether to hold air or let it go. Diego's hand moved from my waist to my back, like he wasn't sure if touching me would help or break me more. He bent slightly to meet my eyes.

I swallowed, throat tight.

"That was …" I breathed out. A beat. "That was Sophie's dad." Diego stilled. His brows pulled together as his thumb brushed a small, grounding circle against my spine. "He hasn't been around in years," I added quickly, like I needed him to know the truth before the panic stole my voice. "He just … he disappeared. And now he's here, married, and I—" My breath hitched. Diego didn't interrupt. He just stepped closer, offering quiet, steady presence.

"I'm right here," he said softly.

I blinked hard as reality sank in, the shock of the moment clashing with old hurt. "I'm fine," I tried, but even I didn't believe it.

He shook his head gently, brushing my cheek with the back of his fingers. "You don't have to be."

"I wasn't expecting him. Not here. Not … now."

"I know." His voice was velvet-soft. "You don't owe me explanations right this second. We can talk upstairs. Or sit for a minute. Whatever you need."

I nodded, swallowing the lump in my throat. Brad's absence had always been a wound, but Diego's presence felt like safety wrapped in a warm weighted blanket.

"I'm okay," I whispered, more certain this time. "I just wasn't prepared. But that's all in the past. I don't want him to be part of this moment."

Diego's chest rose with a quiet breath, like my reassurance meant more to him than he expected it to. "Come here," he said softly. And when I stepped into his arms, everything in me unclenched just a little. His hand moved up to cradle the back of my head, his chin resting against my hair as his breath steadied mine. After a long, quiet moment, he pulled back just enough to look at me.

"Do you want to go upstairs?" he asked quietly.

I nodded. "Yeah. I think I need a minute."

He laced our fingers together. "Okay."

The elevator ride was quiet as Diego stayed close beside me, our fingers intertwined, his thumb brushing gently against my hand the entire ride up. When we stepped into my room, I went straight to the edge of the bed and sat down, exhaling the breath I'd been holding since the lobby. Diego stayed near the door for a moment, giving me space, before coming to sit beside me. He didn't touch me yet, not until I lifted my gaze to his. Only then did he reach for my hand.

"Talk to me," he said softly.

I swallowed, emotions finally loosening enough to spill.

"That was the first time I've seen him since Sophie was a baby," I said quietly. "He just … walked out of our lives. No explanation. And seeing him tonight—" My voice cracked. Diego's jaw tightened just slightly, but his eyes stayed gentle. He scooted closer until our knees touched.

"You don't deserve that. Sophie didn't deserve that. He's a coward, Amelia. Anyone can make a baby. Not everyone steps up to be a parent."

I blinked hard, chest tightening. "I know it shouldn't matter. I don't want him. I don't miss him. But seeing him look at me like I was nothing …" I shook my head. "It hurt, not for me, but for her."

Diego reached up, brushing his thumb gently along my cheek.

"Of course it hurt," he murmured. "You're a good mom. And good people get hurt when bad people make selfish choices." He took a slow breath. "But don't ever confuse his failure with your worth. You and Sophie deserved better. You deserve someone who stays." His voice dropped even softer. "I want to be that person." He didn't say it like a promise he couldn't keep. He said it like something he'd already decided. My breath hitched. "You don't have to say anything right now. I need you to know it. I'm here. And I'm not going anywhere."

Something inside me finally eased, like a fist unclenching after holding on too tight for too long. I leaned into him, resting my forehead against his. The tension in my body softened, my heartbeat syncing with the calm rhythm of his.

I moved before he could say another word. Something in me ignited like a flame. I jumped up to grab his face, kissing him hard, all need and adrenaline and emotion. Diego reacted instantly, his hands gripping my waist, pulling me into him as he needed me just as much. He lifted me off the floor in one strong motion, my legs instinctively wrapping around his waist even through my jeans. The surprised groan in his chest sent a shiver through me.

"Amelia ..." he breathed against my mouth, already losing control. "Are you sure?"

"Yes." I kissed him again, harder. That was all he needed. He laid me onto the bed with a gentleness that didn't match the fire in his eyes, then pulled his shirt over his head—fast, like he'd been waiting months to do it. And God, he looked unreal. All sharp lines and warm skin and abs so defined they looked carved. My breath caught, and his mouth curved into a slow, knowing smile.

"You're staring," he murmured.

"Can you blame me?" I whispered.

He leaned down, kissing me again, deeper this time. His hands slipped beneath my top, sliding it upward, and I raised my arms without a second thought. The second the fabric hit the floor; his hands were on my skin.

I tugged him closer, wanting more of him, all of him. He inhaled sharply when I shifted, rolling him onto his back and straddling him, my palms pressed against the solid heat of his chest. In a heartbeat, his cock found my entrance, soaked and ready for him. Neither of us cared about the protection that night. We needed each other as close as possible ... with no barriers in between us. I let out a small, muffled moan, my eyes rolling into the back of my skull.

"*Dios mío* ..." he whispered, voice low and rough. "You're going to ruin me."

I bent down and kissed him again, and the world narrowed to heat and breath and the way he pulled me closer like he couldn't get enough.

Everything else vanished. There was just him and me as I moved on top of him, breathing heavily as we both chased our peaks.

Just him.

Just me.

And everything between us finally broke open.

Twenty-Three
Amelia

Morning light spilled across the room in soft, golden streaks, warming my skin before I even opened my eyes. For a moment, there was only quiet, warm sheets, a slow inhale behind me, and the weight of an arm draped around my waist.

Diego.

I blinked awake and turning just enough to see him. His hair was tousled, his lips soft with sleep, a single curl resting over his brow. He looked peaceful, completely unguarded in a way that made something inside me flutter.

He stirred when I moved, pulling me closer without fully waking, his nose brushing my shoulder. A soft, sleepy sound escaped him, half Spanish, half sigh.

"*Buenos días, amor,*" he murmured against my skin.

"Good morning," I whispered, smiling.

He opened his eyes slowly, and the second he saw me, as if remembering all at once where we were, his whole expression softened. He leaned forward and kissed my cheek, then my lips, slow and warm.

"I could wake up like this every day," he said, voice rough with sleep.

Heat crept up my neck. "Me too."

He stretched out dramatically and dropped back to the pillows. "I'm starving. Should we order room service?"

I laughed. "Absolutely."

Ten minutes later, breakfast arrived: pancakes, eggs, bacon, fresh fruit, and a pot of coffee that smelled like pure heaven. We sat cross-legged on the bed, eating off each other's plates, laughing when Diego tried to feed me strawberries like we were starring in our own cheesy rom-com. It felt like something I could get used to until his phone buzzed.

His hand paused midway to his coffee cup. He glanced at the caller ID, and his expression shifted.

"Sorry," he said softly. "It's my agent."

He stepped toward the window as he answered. Though I didn't try to listen, pieces of the conversation drifted to me anyway.

"Yeah, I'm here … Okay, slow down … England?" A heavy breath. "We have a month? … I'll think about it."

England.

My stomach tightened in a quiet twist of nerves. Diego slipped his phone back into his pocket and exhaled slowly as he returned to the room.

I swallowed, not wanting to ask too many questions, but unable to ignore what I had heard. "That sounded … serious."

He nodded, coming to sit beside me on the bed. "My agent. There's a transfer window coming up."

My heart tightened. "Okay …"

"A team in England reached out," he said gently. "They're interested. It's early, and nothing is decided. My agent wants me to think about it, and I have about a month to give them an answer."

"A month," I echoed, the words landing heavily.

"I didn't know that call was coming today. But I need you to hear me clearly ..." His thumb brushed my palm, slow and steady. "This doesn't mean I'm leaving you. It doesn't mean I'm choosing my career over us."

I looked down, breathing through the knot in my chest. "It's England, Diego. That's huge."

"I know. But so are you." His voice was so gentle it unraveled something inside me.

"I'm not asking you to decide anything tonight," he said. "But if I do take it, I'd like you to think about whether you'd consider moving there—both of you. I'll make it work. I'll make sure Sophie has a good school and a good home. Everything she needs."

My breath shook. "My life is in Houston. My job. My family. Sophie's routines ..."

"And I respect that," he said immediately. "I'm not expecting you to uproot your life overnight." He leaned in, lifting my chin so I had to meet his eyes. "I'm telling you because I love you. And because you're not a part of my life anymore, you're the center of it."

My chest went tight. It was full, overwhelming, and terrifying in the sweetest way. He wasn't asking me to chase him or giving me ultimatums. He was choosing me, openly and fully.

He cupped my cheek, voice almost breaking. "I'm so in love with you it scares the hell out of me. I can't be without you anymore. Not after this, and not after everything we've been through since we met. I don't want a life that doesn't have you in it."

A tear slipped down my cheek before I could stop it. I leaned my forehead against his, breathing him in. "I'm scared. I don't know what the right choice is."

"That's alright. You don't have to know, right now. Not tonight. Not tomorrow. We have time."

I nodded, feeling the truth settle somewhere deep. "But I'm not running."

His eyes softened. "Good, because wherever my life goes … wherever *our* life goes, I want it with you. Always with you." He pulled me into his chest, and I let myself sink into him, letting his warmth chase away the last pieces of fear clinging to me. And there, wrapped in his arms, the future uncertain but the love impossibly clear, I finally felt it.

We'd figure it out. Together.

Even as we packed our bags, neither of us said much. We didn't need to. Every glance and every brush of his hand against mine felt like its own conversation.

By noon, we were in the back of a taxi heading to the airport. I rested my head on Diego's shoulder; our fingers tangled on the seat between us. He kept lifting my hand to kiss my knuckles, like he needed the reassurance of touch just as much as I did.

"You sure you're, okay?" he asked softly.

"I'm okay. Just thinking."

"About England?"

"About everything."

He exhaled and tucked a loose strand of hair behind my ear. "We'll figure it out," he said again—not as a promise, but as a steady truth. "One step at a time."

The car pulled up to the terminal. Passengers rushed around us, dragging suitcases, checking screens, and saying their own goodbyes. It felt strange that everyone else's lives were moving so fast when ours felt suspended in one long, quiet breath.

Diego walked me to my gate first. I didn't want to let go of his hand. Neither did he.

"When do you get back to Miami?" I asked, trying to sound casual.

"In a couple of hours." He brushed his thumb along my jaw, slow and warm. "And the second I land, I'll let you know."

A small smile tugged at my lips. "Okay."

He leaned his forehead against mine, breathing me in like he needed to memorize this moment before the world tilted again.

"I love you, Amelia," he murmured.

Heat rushed to my chest. It didn't feel like that sensation would ever stop, no matter how many times he said it. "I love you too."

"Text me when you land," he said.

"I will."

"And if you need anything—"

"I know," I whispered, reaching up to gently stroke his cheek.

His eyes softened. "Go," he said gently. "Before I drag you back with me."

I laughed, then kissed him once more—a quick, lingering goodbye that tasted like promise. Then I turned toward my gate. I didn't look back.

Not because I didn't want to, but because for once, I wasn't afraid he wouldn't be there when I turned around.

Twenty-Four
Diego

Airports were nothing new to me.

I'd moved through them my entire adult life: boarding passes, gates, hotels, matches, and different cities. I had always been moving, always in motion. But today felt different. It felt heavy.

I watched Amelia walk toward her gate, her carry-on rolling behind her, her hair falling over her shoulder. She didn't look back, and somehow, that hit me more than if she had, because she trusted I would still be here. She trusted *us*.

When she disappeared into the stream of passengers, I exhaled slowly and turned toward my terminal.

"Bro." Taije jogged up beside me, backpack slung over one shoulder, hat pulled low, the same smug grin he'd had since he helped orchestrate Amelia's surprise.

"Well?" he said, eyebrows raised. "How was your night with Amelia?"

I shook my head, unable to stop the smile tugging at my mouth. "It was good."

"Good?" He scoffed. "Man, please. I saw her walk into the hotel last night. That woman was glowing. And you look like you slept for the first time in three years. Don't give me this 'good' nonsense."

I huffed out a laugh. "Alright. It was amazing."

His grin softened into something knowing. "She's a special girl, Diego. You know that, right?"

"Yeah," I said quietly. "I know."

He studied me for a beat, the humor fading from his face as he really looked at me. "So why do you look like you're thinking about taxes?"

I swallowed. My jaw tightened. With the call, my agent, England, and Amelia roaming through my mind, my head was a mess. The thoughts rumbled all at once.

"Yeah," I muttered. "I'm thinking."

"About what?" he asked, arms crossed. "And don't say 'nothing.' I helped set up that whole damn surprise. I know something is up."

I took a long breath, staring past him at the planes landing outside. Their engines hummed low, heat waves rising off the tarmac. "Benny called this morning." The shift on Taije's face shifted instantly. He knew that, if my agent called, it must have been serious.

"And?"

"A Premier League team reached out."

His eyebrows shot up. "Wait—like *Premier* League?"

"Yeah."

"Holy shit." He let out a low whistle. "That's ... bro, that's insane. That's your dream. That's every kid's dream."

"I know."

"So why do you look like someone told you bad news?"

I dragged a hand through my hair. "Because it's complicated now."

"How?"

I didn't dodge it. "Amelia. And Sophie. For the first time in my life, I can't just pick up my things and leave, because I have something to lose."

Understanding flickered in his eyes. "Ah," he said quietly. "Okay."

"I'm in love with her," I said simply. There were no theatrics or hesitation, just the truth.

"Yeah. I could tell."

"I don't want to lose her," I continued. "And I don't want to give up the chance I've worked for since I was a kid. I want both. And I don't know how this works if England becomes real."

"That's real," he said softly. "But it's not impossible."

"It is," I murmured. "And it's terrifying."

"What did she say when you told her?"

"She's scared," I admitted. "But she didn't pull away. She said we'd figure it out, and that meant everything."

Taije clapped my shoulder. "Then you're fine. You two are grown. You'll make it work. Premier League or not—"

Before he could finish, the overhead speaker chimed. "First class, now boarding."

"That's us," Taije said, grabbing his bag. "Come on."

We walked toward the gate together, and for the first time since the call, my thoughts didn't feel scattered. I stepped aside before boarding to check my phone one last time. A message lit up the screen.

Amelia:

About to take off. Miss you already.

Me:

Miss you more. Call me when you land.

I powered off my phone and followed Taije down the jet bridge. Dreams, fear, and love all mixed together inside me, but one thing stayed clear. She wasn't something I had to choose *instead* of my career. She was the reason I wanted to get it right.

Twenty-Five
Amelia

I still couldn't believe what I had done because it was unlike anything I had ever dared to do before. I'd flown to Arizona to surprise a man I loved, and he hadn't disappointed me.

Not even the shock of seeing Brad in the hotel lobby could ruin what Diego and I shared. If anything, it made me prouder of myself because I didn't let the past decide how I showed up for my present.

Now I was back in Houston, driving toward my parents' house to pick up Sophie. The sky washed in late-afternoon gold, and I didn't even mind being trapped in traffic. My body was home, but my heart remained somewhere in a hotel room.

My phone lit up in the cupholder.

Victoria:

HELLO??? Answer your phone. This is an EMERGENCY. We need DETAILS.

Before I could even smile, the screen lit up again.

Anastasia:

Call us. Now. Victoria's been pacing like a dad in a '90s sitcom.

I shook my head, laughing under my breath, and tapped the call icon on the steering wheel.

"Finally!" Victoria shrieked the moment the line connected.

"You were supposed to call us *last night*," Anastasia added, sounding dramatic and personally offended.

"I literally landed an hour ago," I said through a laugh. "Calm down."

"No," Victoria snapped. "Start talking. Did he faint? Did he scream? Did he pass out in Taije's arms?"

I rolled my eyes, heat rushing to my cheeks. "He was shocked. Like, genuinely stunned."

"I knew it!" Anastasia shouted.

"And then?" Victoria demanded.

"And then it was perfect," I admitted softly, the memory warming me from the inside out. "We talked. We spent the night together. It was everything." First, there was silence; then they both screamed, loud, high-pitched, and borderline feral.

I flinched, laughing. "Okay, okay, I get it …" I let out a small sigh, then, not knowing how to break the news to the girls. "There was … one thing," I said.

Victoria inhaled sharply. "What do you mean by one thing?"

"Brad was there," I said quietly. "At the hotel."

Two beats of stunned silence.

"I'm sorry, *what?*" Anastasia barked.

"Why the hell was *he* in Arizona?" Victoria demanded. "No. Actually. Why was he on the same planet as you?"

I let out a slow breath. "I don't know. He just appeared, but nothing happened. I didn't let him ruin it. I handled it."

"Oh my God," Anastasia muttered. "Okay. We're circling back to that later."

"Later," I echoed, relief smoothing into my voice. "I'm pulling into my parents' driveway."

"Fine," Victoria sighed dramatically. "Go be a mom. But tonight, we expect a full debrief. Charts. Graphics. A recap video."

"Shut up," I laughed.

"We love you," Anastasia added. "And we're proud of you."

I swallowed. "I love you both too."

Minutes later, I turned into my parents' driveway. Sophie saw me through the front window and burst out the door before I could unbuckle. Her curls were wild, glitter clips everywhere, her cheeks flushed with excitement.

"Mommy!" she yelled, launching herself into my arms. I hugged her tight, breathing her in: the scent of crayons, shampoo, and the safe little world we'd built together. *This was home.* It always would be.

My phone buzzed again in my hand.

Diego:

Made it home, amor. I already miss you.

Warmth spread through me like a slow burn. Everything felt like it was shifting, but in the best way.

Monday came fast. I walked into Elite Source in black slacks and a soft blouse, fueled by on a cup of mediocre coffee and the weekend's lingering glow. The office hummed with phones ringing, keyboards tapping, and Lisa waving at me with her usual bright smile from behind her desk.

Life snapped back into place, but something inside me felt different. Softer. Opened. Hopeful.

"Amelia?" Mr. Thompson called from his doorway. "Got a minute?"

"Of course," I said as I followed him inside and sat, notepad in hand.

He wasted no time as he settled into his chair again. "You've been doing exceptional work," he began. "Reliable. Strategic. Clients trust you. Your leadership on the Lumera Beauty campaign was impressive."

Warmth bloomed in my chest. "Thank you." It was nice to get praise for a job well done, even after all these years I've been working for him.

He continued, "We're expanding and want you to step into a more senior role. It's strategy-focused, client-facing, and closer to a director track. It comes with a raise. And a performance bonus." I blinked, stunned. This was everything I'd worked for. "There's one thing," he added gently. "It'll require more hours. More presence. Less flexibility."

My stomach tightened. Less travel meant less time with Diego.

"I know it's a lot," he said. "Take some time to think about it, just let me know soon."

I nodded, overwhelmed. "Thank you. Really."

Back at my desk, Lisa slid in as if she'd been waiting for the moment my door closed.

"Okay," she whispered loudly. "Your face is saying something big just happened."

I let out a slow exhale. "He offered me a new position."

Her eyes widened. "Like *the* position? The one they hinted at last year?" I nodded. She smacked my arm lovingly. "Amelia! That's huge!"

"I know. It feels unreal."

"And terrifying?" she asked knowingly. I didn't answer. She already knew. Lisa softened. "What's holding you back? Sophie? Or Miami Boy?"

I swallowed. "Both, maybe."

She nudged my arm again. "Look. Whatever you choose, you'll make it work. You always do."

I smiled weakly. "I'll think about it."

After work, I picked up Sophie from my parents' house and let her ramble about her day while I cooked dinner. I held her tighter tonight than usual, her curls brushing my cheek as she climbed into my lap to show me a drawing she had made at school.

When she finally fell asleep, I curled up in bed with my phone in hand, waiting for Diego's name to light up on my screen.

It didn't take long.

Diego:

How was your day today, amor?

Me:

Good. But a lot. I got offered a new role with my company. A big one.

He video called me almost immediately. His face popped up, and I couldn't help but smile at the sight of him.

"Tell me everything," he said, voice warm and grounding.

I exhaled. "It's a huge step. Higher position. More responsibility. More hours. And a lot less flexibility."

"Wow," he said softly. "That's incredible. I'm proud of you. You should go out and celebrate. I wish I were closer so I could make that happen." The smile still lingered on his face, and the praise warmed my chest, but I felt a shift in him anyway. Something was happening. I could tell. He likely just didn't want to steal my spotlight.

"What is it?" I asked. He went to shake his head, but I continued, "We'll make it work. Whatever it is."

"The England offer," he said. "My agent keeps pushing. The club wants an answer sooner than I expected."

A lump tightened in my throat. "Are you leaning one way?"

He hesitated just long enough to make my breath catch. "I want to talk to you first," he admitted. "I meant what I said in Phoenix. If I make this move, I want to do it with you. I want you *with* me." My heart thudded painfully. "We don't have to decide anything tonight. I just wanted you to know where things stand." Silence wrapped around us for a moment before he spoke again. "I miss you."

"I miss you too."

"And whatever happens," he said, "I just want the best for Sophie and for us."

My chest tightened. Love and fear were all tangled up, but this time, I didn't let myself run.

"I'll think about everything," I whispered. "I just need time."

"You have it," he promised. "I'm right here."

We stayed like that for a few seconds, breathing into the quiet, neither of us wanting to hang up first. Eventually, the call ended, and the screen went dark. I sat in the stillness of my room, my heart full and heavy at the same time.

England.

The word pulsed in my mind like a faraway lighthouse. Not here yet, but close enough to cast a faint glow over everything. I didn't know what my life would look like if I moved across an ocean. If Sophie started school in a different country. If I traded the Houston skyline for one I'd only ever seen on postcards. But for the first time, I let myself imagine it.

A small house somewhere quiet. Sophie running in a backyard bursting with flowers she couldn't name. Me working from a cozy little office, building something of my own. Watching Diego on the field … My life turning into something bigger than I ever dreamed it could be.

It was a life I wasn't ready for yet, but maybe someday I would be.

I exhaled, sinking deeper into the pillows as the night pressed warmly against my window.

Whatever came next, I'd figure it out.

I just didn't know the next few days would change everything.

Twenty-Six

Amelia

A couple of days have passed, and somehow life slipped right back into its usual rhythm, morning routines, school drop-offs, late emails, and Sophie's glitter projects scattered all over the kitchen table, but everything felt just a little different. Fuller and quieter in the places that mattered, louder in the ones that made me think too much.

Thursday night arrived with Sophie buzzing at the idea of staying up to watch Miami's game on TV. We curled up on the couch, a blanket wrapped around us, the soft glow of the screen filling the living room. Sophie squealed every time Diego touched the ball, pointing and kicking her legs like her enthusiasm alone could help him score.

"He's so good, Mommy!" she announced proudly, as if she personally trained him. I couldn't help smiling.

"He really is."

When Diego scored, Sophie screamed loud enough that the neighbors probably heard her. She jumped up, danced, then flopped back beside me, breathless.

"Can we call him after?" She asked with such earnest hope that my heart tightened.

"We can try," I said softly.

By the time the match ended, she was half-asleep, curled into my side. I carried her to bed, kissed her forehead, and stood in her doorway for a long moment, letting the calm settle.

Later, Diego video called me from the locker room hallway, still in his kit, hair damp, eyes bright.

"Did you watch the game?" he asked, already smiling.

"We did," I said. "Sophie cheered. A lot." His laugh filled my chest with something steady and warm. We didn't talk about decisions, mine or his. Just the little things. The good things. The kind that made you feel like the world might actually be working in your favor.

When we hung up, I felt the quiet more sharply than before.

Tomorrow, I thought to myself. *I'll decide everything tomorrow.*

Friday morning, the office buzzed with its usual back-to-back chaos. Phones ringing, printers whining, coworkers weaving through hallways with half-finished coffees. I walked in feeling both grounded and suspended at the same time. Lisa practically skipped to my desk.

"You look zen," she said with suspicion.

I laughed. "I'm really not."

"You're deciding today, aren't you?"

I nodded once.

Her expression softened. "Whatever you choose, you'll kill it. But personally," she leaned in conspiratorially. "I hope you take the promotion. You're ready."

Maybe I was. By mid-morning, I stepped into Mr. Thompson's office with my decision already settled firm in my chest.

"I'd like to accept the position," I told him.

He nodded, pleased. "Good. It fits you." His confidence steadied me more than I expected.

Work moved fast after that: meetings, introductions, responsibilities being handed to me. It felt big and right, but it also felt like taking a step deeper into a life I'd built, brick by brick. A life that didn't exactly make it easy to follow someone across an ocean.

That evening, I picked up Sophie from school, her backpack bouncing against her legs.

"Mommy! Nana said I can sleep over again!" She grinned, missing one front tooth. *Of course she could.*

I dropped her off at my parents' house after dinner and watched her run straight into my mom's arms. My dad waved from the living room. My mom squeezed my shoulder the way she always did when she sensed I was holding too much inside.

"You okay, sweetheart?" she whispered.

"Yeah," I said. "Just tired." maybe a little lost. And that was about it.

Heading home alone felt strange, like walking into a version of my life that didn't quite fit anymore.

Inside, I kicked off my shoes, dropped my keys on the counter, and stood in the soft quiet of my living room, thinking about the promotion, about Sophie, about Diego's voice saying, *"I'm right here."*

What would life look like if I stayed? What would it look like if I didn't? I didn't have the answers yet. But for the first time, both futures felt possible.

I was halfway lost in those thoughts when the doorbell rang. It was too late for a delivery. Too early for Victoria or Anastasia. And Diego was thousands of miles away.

I stepped toward the door slowly, each footstep louder than the last.

When I opened it, my breath froze.

Brad.

My mouth fell open, but no words came. I stared, my eyes tracing the familiar lines of his face in disbelief. I had seen him in passing, yes, but that was an encounter I never expected to repeat. Certainly not here, not like this, not on my doorstep.

"Hey, Millie," he said softly. It was what he used to call me, back when everything between us was different, before he had completely shattered my heart. The sound of it sent a rush of conflicting emotions through me. Brad shifted, his eyes on me as the silence stretched between us. And then, he asked, "Can I come inside?"

Unsure of what else to do, I stepped aside, moving before my mind could catch up. Brad walked past me into the apartment, his shoulders slightly hunched, his hands shoved deep into his pockets. He didn't say anything at first. His eyes wandered slowly, drifting across the room as though he was trying to memorize a place he didn't belong in anymore.

His gaze lingered on the countless photos framed on the walls and shelves—pictures of Sophie smiling, laughing, growing. Pictures of me holding her, just the two of us, building a life that had nothing to do with him. Toys were scattered around the living room, like little reminders of the world Sophie and I had made together. That was a whole world he had chosen to walk away from.

At last, his eyes shifted back to me. He stood still, silent for a beat too long, as though unsure of how to bridge the chasm between us.

"How have you been?" he finally asked.

I blinked at him; sure, I must have misheard him. My mind took a full moment to catch up with the absurdity of his words.

"Are you serious right now?" I said at last, shaking my head slowly. "You disappear for five years—*five years*—and this is how you show up? This is what you choose to ask me?" My eyebrows lifted in sheer astonishment, my chest tightening with anger and confusion. "*Unbelievable.*"

"That's fair enough," he murmured, though it sounded like he was speaking more to himself than to me. His jaw tightened, and in a few long steps, he closed the space between us until he was standing directly in front of me.

"Look," he began, his tone low, "I know I broke your heart. I know I was an absolute asshole"—*an understatement if there ever was one*— "and I know I made life for you and Sophie so unbearably hard. I've spent years thinking about that, years trying to figure out how I could make things right."

I folded my arms tightly across my chest. Every instinct in me screamed to tell him to get the hell out of my home and my life for good. But another voice reminded me of the truth I couldn't ignore.

He was Sophie's father. And whether I wanted to hear him or not, she deserved at least that I give him a chance to speak.

"I've been thinking about Sophie. About you. More often than I want to admit," he continued, his words careful, as though each one cost him something. "I was young back then. I didn't—"

"I was young too, Brad," I cut him off sharply. My voice trembled, not with weakness but with the storm of emotions threatening to spill over. "I was just as scared as you were. I had no idea what I was doing, but when we agreed to have our baby, I expected—no, I *needed*—to be able to rely on you. I thought I could count on you to stand beside me through it all." My throat tightened, but the words kept coming, raw and unstoppable. "I should have known better, though," I said bitterly, shaking my head. "Anastasia told me. Victoria told me. They both said you weren't good for me. But I didn't listen. I defended you because I wanted so badly to make us work. Like a fool, I fought for a man who didn't care about me or our daughter.

"I know," Brad said quietly, his voice carrying an unusual weight. "And I admire what you've done. I admire how you raised Sophie and everything you've managed to achieve on your own. I'm only sorry I wasn't here to see it."

His words lingered in my mind, circling like an echo I couldn't chase away. What was happening right now? The Brad I once knew had been immature, reckless, and selfish. Toxic and pushy in ways I hadn't even recognized back then, too blind and too desperate to make things work. I hadn't seen it clearly in those days, but as the years passed and I built a life on my own, the truth became undeniable. He hadn't been a partner. He had been a burden.

And yet, standing in front of me now, he didn't look like the same boy who had broken me. Could he have grown, too? Could he have changed? The thought unsettled me. I wasn't anywhere close to forgiving him, and I wasn't even considering letting him near Sophie, but part of me wondered if life had humbled him in ways I couldn't see yet.

"It was your choice," I said finally. I took a step back, putting space between us. "Not mine."

Brad ran a hand through his short hair, his eyes dropping for a moment as he gave a small, almost regretful nod. "I know. I'm not denying that. I messed everything up, and I have a lot to make up for." He paused, his words careful. "But I was just wondering if you'd at least give me the chance. I want to see Sophie. I want to be involved in her life. I want to—"

"Absolutely not." The words left me before he could even finish—I cut him off without hesitation. I could deal with the scars he had left me. I could live with the heartbreak, the abandonment, and the nights I cried myself to sleep because I had no one to lean on but myself. I had survived all of it, but I would never let my daughter go through the same thing.

She didn't even remember him. She had been so small when he first held her, too little to form any memory of the man standing in front of me now. Since then, he hadn't tried. Not once. He hadn't called. He hadn't visited. He hadn't written. He had chosen absence, and Sophie had grown up without knowing a father.

And truthfully, that was for the best. She was thriving. She was loved. She was safe. My daughter didn't need a man who thought he could step in and out of her life whenever it suited him. I wasn't going to give him the chance to shatter her the way he had shattered me.

"Millie, please, I want to—"

"Stop calling me that!" I snapped. Something inside me twisted hard, and my heart began pounding so fast it felt like it would burst out of my chest. "I told you—*no*. Sophie is not a toy you pull out when it suits you. She's a little girl who needs constancy, safety, and a father she can rely on. If you've shown me anything, it's that I can't trust you to give her those thing ."

His mouth opened as if to speak, and he tried, "But I've changed, and I want to—"

"I can't know that!" I cut him off before he could finish. "I don't get to gamble on your promises. I can't risk her being hurt the way you hurt me. You shattered my heart, Brad, and I will not let you break hers."

For a long, heavy moment, he stood there in silence, his eyes on me as if he were gathering the next thing to say from the floor. Then, quietly, he said, "But I'm her father. I have rights. Dora and I are trying to expand our family. She wants children, and when she found out—"

Those words hit me hard. The room tilted for a second, and my legs nearly gave out under the rush of anger and disbelief. *Of course.* Of course, that was why he was here. Not because he missed Sophie or wanted to make amends, but because he sought something that would make him look better and offer a new version of a life he could present.

"Get out. Get out right now!" I shouted, the words tearing out of me. The neighbors might have heard, but I didn't care. I needed him gone from my home, gone from my life, and gone from the small, safe world I'd built for Sophie and me. He didn't care about my daughter. He didn't care about what he had done to us. He wanted an accessory for his life and someone to fill a role when it suited him. That was all.

He opened his mouth again, voice sharp with entitlement. "I have rights, and I will—"

"Get. Out." I warned him, the fury in my eyes plain and scorching. I wanted him to understand I meant it. He hesitated, then took a long step back, but not without a final, ugly motion, he lifted a finger as if to wag at me.

"This is not over, Amelia. Do you hear me? This is not over. I'll get what I want."

Twenty-Seven
Amelia

"What the hell do you mean Brad came to visit you?"

Victoria's voice was sharper and louder than usual, almost breaking as she stared at me with wide eyes. Her face turned a deep shade of red, and she clenched her fists at her sides. She was *furious*, and that was the kind of anger I hadn't seen from her since Brad first walked out on me and Sophie.

Back then, I had tried everything to get him to stay in touch for Sophie's sake. I called, texted, and even sent letters, hoping he would care enough to be part of her life but he didn't. He didn't want anything to do with us. After months of trying, I finally stopped. I accepted that he was gone for good. I had even grown okay with that arrangement, even.

And now, suddenly, he was back, acting like he had a say in things he had long abandoned.

"Are you okay?" Anastasia asked quietly, stepping closer and taking my hand. Her touch was warm and gentle, but it only made the lump in my throat feel heavier.

Last night still felt like a blur. My thoughts had been spinning so fast that I barely slept. I tossed and turned until morning, replaying every word Brad had said. When I finally got up, I called my best friends and asked if they could come over. Before that. I had asked my mom to keep Sophie for a little longer, saying I had some errands to run. I couldn't bring myself to explain the real reason.

Was I okay? That was the question I didn't have an answer to. My chest felt tight, and I could barely breathe, but I still forced myself to nod, pretending I was fine. I didn't want them to worry more than they already did.

"Yeah. I just … I needed someone to talk to. I don't know what to do. Should I get a lawyer? Should I call the police? What am I supposed to do?" The words rushed out before I could stop them. Panic rose inside me, threatening to pull me under.

Anastasia wrapped her arm around me, pulling me into a soft hug. Victoria stood there with her arms crossed, her brows drawn together as if she were trying to come up with a plan.

"I don't think the police can help right now," she finally said. "They'll probably say their hands are tied because he hasn't done anything yet. It's ridiculous." She sighed and pressed her fingers to the bridge of her nose, as if trying to chase away the stress building there. "You could talk to a lawyer, though, just in case. But honestly, I don't think Brad will follow through on anything. He never sticks with anything that takes effort, and we both know that."

She was right. Brad was all talk and no action. And after everything he'd done, my friends probably knew him just as well as I did.

Anastasia slowly let go of me, stepping back to meet my eyes. "Seriously, Amelia, I think his only goal is to scare you and stir up trouble in your life. That's what Brad does best.

Maybe he saw those pictures of you and Diego going around online, and now he's trying to ruin things for you. Don't let him do that."

A shiver ran through me, and my stomach twisted as I tried to take it all in. She might've been right. It did feel like Brad was trying to get under my skin, like he had some plan I couldn't quite figure out. And that uncertainty terrified me more than anything else.

I knew one thing, either way. Whatever his intentions were, I had to be prepared for them.

The weekend passed quietly. I couldn't stand being at home, not by myself and not even with Sophie. The walls felt like they were closing in, so I packed a small bag and drove to my parents' house. My mom seemed a little surprised to see me at the door, but she didn't ask questions. Maybe she sensed that I needed this, or maybe she didn't want to push. Either way, I was grateful. I didn't have the strength to explain what was really going on. If I told her, she'd worry, and I couldn't handle her worry on top of my own.

"Mommy, are you okay?" Sophie's soft voice broke through my thoughts as we drove home on Monday afternoon. Her question pulled me out of the fog that had settled over me since Friday. I blinked and caught her eyes in the rearview mirror.

Usually, this would've been our favorite part of the day—the car ride home filled with her stories about school, her friends, and whatever new trend she was obsessed with that week. But today, the silence between us felt heavy, so I understood why she asked.

I forced a small smile. "Of course, pumpkin. I've just had a long day at work, that's all. I'm a little tired."

She tilted her head, watching me carefully. "Are you sure? You look sad."

My heart squeezed. How did I end up with a child who was so perceptive and emotionally aware? Between Brad and Diego's potential transfer to England, it felt like I was stretched thin. Still, I couldn't help the tiny laugh that escaped me. "I'm sure, sweetheart. Really. I'm just tired. But enough about me, how about you tell me how many bracelets we have to make tonight?"

That did the trick. Her face lit up instantly, and she launched into a story about the bracelets she and her friends were planning to trade at school. Her laughter filled the car, and for the first time in days, I felt something close to peace.

The rest of the drive slipped by easily, but when we pulled into the driveway, that peace shattered in an instant. I spotted a familiar, unwanted figure. Brad stood at our doorstep. He was holding a bouquet in one hand and a teddy bear in the other, wearing what I assumed was meant to be apologetic.

Sophie stood beside me, her small hand clutching mine as she stared at him for a long moment. Her little face scrunched up, clearly unsure what to make of the man in front of us. The last time she had seen Brad, she had been far too young to remember. Now, he was just a stranger standing at our doorstep with flowers and a stuffed bear, pretending to be someone he wasn't.

A dull ache began to build behind my eyes as I tried to steady my breathing and keep calm. Every part of me wanted to turn around, take Sophie inside, and lock the door behind us, but I knew I had to handle this carefully.

I looked down at her and forced a soft smile. "How about you go inside and get yourself some ice cream, sweetheart?" I said, keeping my tone light. "I'll be right in after you."

Instantly, her face lit up, her earlier confusion replaced by excitement. Ice cream always worked—it was my secret weapon whenever I needed her distracted. "Really?" she asked, already bouncing on her toes.

"Really," I said with a nod.

Without needing to be told twice, she hurried toward the door. I didn't bother to introduce her to Brad, but being the polite little girl she was, she turned and gave him a shy wave before disappearing inside. That simple, innocent gesture nearly broke me. Emotion surged through my chest, threatening to erupt, but I pushed it down and turned to face Brad.

"I thought I made myself clear the last time we talked," I said quietly, mindful of the neighbours around us.

He scoffed, his expression hardening. "Yeah, you said plenty. But I also know you love Sophie, just like I do." My whole body tensed. The way he said her name made my skin crawl. I could tell he was trying to sound sincere, but his words were hollow. "I want to try again," he continued. "I want you to give me another chance, so I can make things right. I want—"

"I don't care what you want, Brad," I interrupted, my voice sharper now. "You walked away years ago. You left me and Sophie to pick up the pieces. Now you show up out of nowhere, acting like you're owed something. You're not. You don't get to know her. Not now. When she turns eighteen, she can make her own choices. But until then, I'm not letting you near *my* daughter."

His fake charm disappeared in an instant. The flowers dropped to the ground, followed by the teddy bear, as his face twisted with anger. He stepped closer, towering over me. My pulse quickened, but I refused to back away. I meant every word, and I wasn't going to let him intimidate me.

"You bitch," he muttered through clenched teeth. made my stomach twist, but I didn't flinch. "You think you can stop me from seeing my daughter?"

I met his glare. "If you try anything, I'll call the police. And if that's not enough, I'll get a restraining order. No judge will grant you visitation rights after everything you've done. You abandoned your child before she was even born, Brad. You don't get to walk back in whenever you want."

For a moment, he was silent. Then a slow, cruel smile spread across his face. It wasn't the smirk I remembered from years ago—it was darker, emptier. And in that instant, I realized something had changed in him. He wasn't the same man who had once broken my heart. *He was worse.*

"Go ahead and try. See where that gets you," Brad said, his tone full of smug confidence. "I have connections everywhere now. You think just because you're dating your soccer boyfriend now, you're untouchable? That you get to decide what I can or can't do? You're wrong." He shook his head. "I know that he's been offered a transfer to England. And I know *you*, so you're more than likely considering taking it so you wouldn't have to let me see my daughter." That wasn't the truth, but the expression on his face terrified me enough to consider it. "If you try to do that, I'll sue you for kidnapping my daughter." I opened my mouth to respond, but he didn't give me the chance. "I know people. Push me hard enough, and I'll make you regret ever being born, let alone trying to keep me away from Sophie."

For a moment, I couldn't even process what he had said. My heart raced, pounding so hard it hurt. His words spun in my head until everything around me blurred. Before I could think, I shoved him backward hard.

And that was a terrible mistake.

The instant my hands touched him, his expression shifted. In one quick motion, he grabbed me by the throat and slammed me back against the wall. My body hit it with a dull thud, the breath ripping from my lungs. His grip tightened around my neck, and fear flooded through me like ice water.

"Don't you ever do that again," he hissed, leaning in close. His eyes burned with a wild, unhinged anger that made my blood run cold. In that moment, I knew Sophie could never see this man. I would do anything, absolutely anything, to keep her safe from him. I tried to tell him to let go, but all that came out was a choked gasp. My vision blurred just as the door next to mine creaked open.

"Everything okay, Amelia?"

The voice came from Mr. Wilson, my elderly neighbor. His gray hair was neatly combed back, and he leaned heavily on his cane as he looked between us with concern. His blue eyes were sharp, alert, ready to step in if needed. *Bless his soul.*

Brad froze. His grip loosened, and he stepped away from me. I stumbled forward, gasping for air, while he bent down and picked up the teddy bear and the flowers he had dropped earlier. Without saying another word, he shoved them into my arms. My hands trembled as I took them automatically, too stunned to react.

"Yes," Brad said smoothly, forcing a smile as he turned toward Mr. Wilson. "Just a misunderstanding." He looked back at me then, his eyes cold and empty. "Think about what I said."

Twenty-Eight
Diego

"Do you plan on telling me what's going on with you?" Taije asked, raising an eyebrow as we walked out of practice. His tone was casual, but his eyes were sharp, studying me the way only a longtime friend could. Usually, we would head to our favorite healthy restaurant after training, but today I wasn't in the mood for it.

I didn't even know how to explain what was bothering me. There wasn't one specific thing I could point to; it was just this uneasy feeling sitting heavy in my chest. Something didn't feel right, and that scared me more than I wanted to admit. Amelia and I had promised each other that we would always face difficult things together and be honest no matter what. I believed her when she said it, so why did I still feel like something was wrong? Like she was slipping away, and I couldn't stop it?

"Everything's fine," I said finally, hoping that would be enough to get him off my back.

Taije gave me a look that told me he wasn't buying a word of it. If there was one person I couldn't lie to, it was him. We had been friends since we were kids, chasing the same dream on the same fields. Now, years later, we were teammates, brothers in every sense except blood. That bond had its perks, but it also meant he could see right through me.

"What is it?" he asked again, his dark eyes locked on mine. "And don't even think about skipping lunch. You know we need protein, and I'm not letting you go home to survive on a protein bar and a sad salad."

I fought the urge to roll my eyes. For someone my age, Taije sure liked to act like a dad sometimes. Most of the time, it was useful, But right now it was just irritating.

"I'll tell you when we sit down," I said, exhaling slowly. "But just so we're clear, this lunch is on you."

He chuckled, shaking his head, and we made our way toward the restaurant. The Miami sun beat down hard, making the pavement shimmer and the air feel heavy. Usually, I didn't mind the heat. I had grown up in it, trained in it, and lived in it for years. Today, though, it only made my restlessness worse.

As we walked, my thoughts drifted back to last night. I had called Amelia to hear her voice. Something in her tone was off. She sounded tired, not just physically but emotionally drained. I asked if everything was okay, but she brushed it off, saying she'd just had a long day.

I wanted to dig deeper and find out what was really wrong, but something in her voice stopped me. That small, quiet part of me that trusted her told me to let it go and believe her word. That was the deal we made, after all. *We would talk when things got hard.*

Still, as I followed Taije into the restaurant, that uneasy feeling in my gut didn't go away. It sat there like a stone, whispering that something was already breaking, even if I couldn't see it yet.

My movements felt automatic as we stepped inside the restaurant. The walls were painted a soft sage green that complemented the calm atmosphere, and the wooden tables and chairs added a warm, earthy feel to the space. Potted plants hung from the ceiling and lined the corners, making it feel more like a garden than a restaurant. Everything about the place reflected its healthy, natural theme, not just in the food they served but in the design itself.

Taije and I ordered our usual: grilled chicken with rice, their signature sauce, and a pile of fresh vegetables. It had been our go-to meal since we first started coming here years ago, back when neither of us could cook much beyond scrambled eggs.

As soon as we sat down, I knew Taije wasn't going to let things slide. He didn't even have to speak. One look at the way his eyebrow lifted told me he wanted answers. He leaned back in his chair, waiting patiently.

"Fine," I muttered, slouching slightly as I let out a slow breath. It wasn't like me to feel so restless, to let something eat at me like this. And it definitely wasn't like me to feel this deeply for someone. But things had changed. *I* had changed. "It's Amelia," I finally admitted. "We had a good conversation the other day, or at least I thought we did. But now it feels like she's pulling away again."

"Have you talked to her about it?" Taije asked, wasting no time getting to the point.

"Well, no, but—"

"Then that's where you need to start," he said firmly. "You're my best friend, and I get that this is new territory for you. You've never liked anyone this much before." The word '*like*' suddenly felt far too small for what I felt for Amelia. It didn't even come close. Taije went on, "I know how you are. You overthink things. You get lost in your own head and start imagining worst-case scenarios instead of asking questions. If you really care about her, and I know you do, you need to talk to her. Don't assume. Just talk."

I raised an eyebrow at him. "When did you get so wise?"

He let out a laugh, shaking his head. "It's not wisdom, man. It's common sense. You should try it sometime." His smirk widened. "So, how about you stop guessing and actually call her?"

I couldn't help but smile at that, even as I reached for my glass of water. I took a long sip, thinking over what he had said. As usual, he was right. I'd been stuck in my own head, worrying instead of acting.

By the time our plates arrived, the smell of grilled chicken and herbs filling the air, I had already made up my mind. I would call Amelia tonight. I needed to hear from her about whatever was bothering her. And maybe I could be there to fix it.

By the time I got home, I felt a little more settled. The conversation with Taije had helped quiet my thoughts, and for the first time all day, I believed that maybe I was overthinking everything. The uneasy feeling I had was probably nothing more than fear now that I had someone to lose.

Nothing had actually happened between us. The truth was simple: I just missed her. Maybe that was all this was about. If we could plan something soon, a quick trip, even just a weekend together, it would make things better. She could visit me, or I could go to her once the season slowed down. That thought alone eased the tension sitting in my chest.

With one of the biggest games of the year coming up, I couldn't leave right now, but once it was over, I promised myself I'd take a few days off. I wanted to spend time with not only Amelia, but also Sophie. There were new tricks I'd been dying to teach her—little soccer moves I knew she'd love.

After a long shower, I changed into something comfortable and sank onto the couch. The apartment was quiet except for the faint hum of the city outside. I grabbed my phone, scrolling to Amelia's contact, and pressed call before I could talk myself out of it.

The line rang once, then twice, then again. Five times. Seven. My stomach tightened as each second dragged on. I was just about to hang up when I finally heard her voice.

"Hello?" she said softly. Something about her tone made my heart drop. It was faint and distant, as if her mind were somewhere far away.

"*Amor?* Are you alright?" I asked carefully.

There was a pause, a long one. I could almost hear her trying to gather herself, and that silence alone made my pulse quicken. I got up and started pacing across the living room, unable to stay still.

"Yeah …" she said finally, her voice hesitant. "Yeah. I'm fine. I have a lot on my plate at the moment. I'm sorry I haven't called, I just …" She trailed off, leaving the sentence hanging in the air between us. The quiet that followed felt heavy.

"That's all right," I said gently. "Do you want to talk about it? What's going on?"

Another pause.

This one lasted even longer, and with every second that passed, the ache in my chest grew sharper. I wanted to reach through the phone and pull her close so I could take whatever was weighing on her and make it disappear.

"I don't think I want to talk about it right now," Amelia said softly, her voice trembling just enough for me to catch it. "Maybe a little later, when everything settles down. I have a lot to do. I need to check in with Sophie's school, and I have to find an apartment and—"

"Wait," I cut her off, my heart skipping a beat. "An apartment? What are you talking about?" The words hit me like a cold shock, and I gripped the phone tighter. "I need you to explain what's happening. Are you moving? What's wrong with your current place?"

There was a pause on the other end of the line. Then she said, "I can't right now … I just can't."

Her tone sent a wave of panic through me. Whatever was going on, it wasn't small. I could hear the strain in her voice, and it was the kind that only came when something was seriously wrong.

"Okay, okay," I said, trying to sound calm even though my chest felt tight. "Just take a deep breath and tell me what's happening. If you're moving, I can help. I can't come right now because of the game, but I can arrange movers or even fly out right after. You don't have to do this alone. Just talk to me. Tell me what's going on so I can help."

That was when I heard it—the sound of her trying to hold back a sob, and then the quiet, broken cry that followed.

The sound of it cracked something inside me. My throat tightened, and I swallowed hard, desperate to keep my own emotions in check.

"It's okay," I said softly, pacing the length of my living room. "Just take your time, baby. I'm here."

There was a shaky breath on the other end. Then, in a voice so small I almost didn't catch it, she said, "I'm probably going to move someplace else. Maybe in the city. Maybe not. I don't know."

The words landed like a punch to the gut. I froze. From the way she said it, I knew England or Miami wasn't where she was headed.

I didn't mind her moving. People moved all the time. But what tore at me was the fact that she hadn't told me or even thought to bring it up before making the decision.

"Okay …" I finally said, dragging out the word, trying to piece my thoughts together. "And you didn't think that was something worth telling me? What happened to us being honest with each other? What happened to giving this a real chance?" I exhaled softly, realizing that the words might've been a little harsher than I wanted them to be. My voice softened as I continued. "I can't be there for you if you don't let me. You know that, right? You know I'd do anything for you. Just talk to me, *mi amor*. Please."

More sobs escaped her then. They were deep, broken sounds that made my stomach twist and my chest ache—the kind of crying that came from somewhere raw and painful. I could barely breathe as fear rushed through me.

"Amelia, please," I said, my voice shaking more than I wanted it to. "Talk to me. What's going on? Did something happen to you? To Sophie?"

But she didn't answer. The only thing I could hear was her loud, uncontrollable, heartbreaking crying. Every sound tore through me, and I felt completely helpless, stuck miles away from the person I wanted most to protect.

"You need to tell me what's happening," I said again, trying to steady my voice even as panic pressed harder against my ribs.

"I can't," she managed to choke out between sobs. "I can't do this. I can't—"

"Can't do what?" My pulse was pounding so fast I thought my chest might explode.

"I can't do this," she repeated, her voice breaking apart. She sounded lost, almost desperate. "I'm sorry. I can't do this right now. I can't. I can't."

"Okay, baby, just calm down. We can talk; we can figure it out—"

"No." Her voice came out sharper this time, more certain. "I can't do this. I can't do us. There's too much …" She trailed off, her words fading into another long silence that felt that twisted deeper with every passing second.

My throat tightened as her meaning sank in. I couldn't even move. It was as if every sound in the world had vanished, leaving me with only the echo of her words. My heart felt like it was tearing itself apart, piece by piece.

"Amelia …" I whispered, forcing the word through the lump in my throat. "Don't do this. Please. Whatever the issue, we can resolve it. Just talk to me."

"I can't," she said finally. "I'm sorry." And then the line went dead.

The silence that followed was unbearable. I stayed frozen where I was, the phone still pressed to my ear long after the call had ended. My mind couldn't process what had just happened. My hands were trembling, and all I could do was stare blankly at the wall across from me.

The ache in my chest was sharp and relentless, like something was ripping me apart from the inside. For the first time in a long time, I didn't know what to do. I didn't even know how to breathe. All I could feel was the emptiness she had left behind.

Twenty-Nine
Diego

I missed practice the next morning and told my coach I wasn't feeling well. I blamed it on food poisoning, but I would have taken that a million times over what I was really dealing with. At least the food poisoning went away after a few hours. Heartbreak didn't.

Amelia broke up with me.

Even thinking about it felt unreal. The words didn't make sense in my head. She hadn't given me a reason or the chance to understand or fight for us. It was over, just like that.

I must have called her a dozen times after that night. Each call went to voicemail, and every message I sent was left unanswered. I kept telling myself there had to be more to it, that something must have happened, something I could help her through if she would just let me in. But she didn't, and the silence was starting to eat away at me.

Lying in bed, I turned onto my back and stared blankly at the ceiling. My muscles ached, but it wasn't the usual soreness from training. This was different. It was a deep, dull pain that settled in my chest and refused to fade. Every thought of her just made it worse.

For the first time in a long time, I felt utterly powerless. There was no play to run, no goal to score, nothing I could do to fix this. She was gone, and I had no idea why. And worse, I was far away from her, so I couldn't even be there for her right now.

I found myself swearing at every wrong step I'd taken along the way. I even found myself reconsidering the offer to move to England. I just couldn't handle the thought of being ever further away from Amelia.

My phone's screen lit up. For a brief moment, I thought it might be her. For some foolish reason, I suspected that she had somehow changed her mind and decided to text me. She didn't.

Taije's name lit up my phone, and I saw the message before I even unlocked it.

Taije:

There's no way that's food poisoning. What's going on? Have you spoken to Amelia?

I stared at the text for a long time. My thumb hovered over the screen. The truth felt heavy in my hand. Finally, after too many seconds, I gave in and typed the one line that burned when I hit send.

Me:

She broke up with me.

His reply came almost immediately, the way it always did when something big hit him.

Taije:

Are you kidding me? What the hell, man? Why?

Saying the words out loud, even in a text, felt like throwing rocks at myself. I tried to soften the following message, but it still felt raw.

Me:

I don't know. She wouldn't say. The whole thing was weird. I guess I have to respect her decision and give her space.

Taije:

She seriously didn't tell you why she broke up with you? That makes no sense. From what Victoria told me about her friends; this is not like Amelia at all.

He was right. None of it matched the Amelia I knew. She would not shut down like that without a reason. For a moment, I let myself believe it was a mistake or something that could be fixed, but then the quiet reality settled back in. If she didn't want to talk, I couldn't force her.

Me:

I know. But she made her decision, and I have to respect it, no matter how hard it is.

Taije:

You know what? I will send you Victoria's number. Contact her. See if she knows anything. But be careful. If you did something, even by accident, be ready. She might get angry at you.

A second later, Victoria's number showed up in the chat. My stomach flipped. Part of me was terrified of what I might hear when I called Amelia's best friend, but the other part could no longer stand the uncertainty. It had only been a day, and it already felt like a year. If this couldn't be fixed, at least I wanted to know why it happened.

I did not give myself time to think it over. I tapped the number and called Victoria. The phone rang a few times, and then someone answered.

"Hello?" she said.

The words rushed out of me before she had a chance to speak. I could feel my voice shaking, and I didn't even try to hide it. "Hey, Victoria, it's Diego. I don't know if you heard, but Amelia broke up with me. She wouldn't tell me why. I don't know if I did something to hurt her. I really don't think I did, but if I did, I want a chance to fight for her. *Please*. I love her, and I want to fight for her." Everything spilled out in a single breath. I waited, heart pounding, for Victoria to say something that might make any of it make sense.

"Fuck …" Victoria swore under her breath, and I could almost hear the frustration dripping from every word. "What the hell is she doing?"

A long, heavy sigh followed, one that told me immediately that Amelia hadn't even mentioned the breakup to her. That only made the pit in my stomach deepen. Something wasn't right. This wasn't about me. It had nothing to do with me. There was something else she was struggling with, something big enough to push her away from me completely.

"So, she didn't tell you?"

"No," Victoria said firmly. "She only told me about Brad. He came over and threatened her. He said that he would take Sophie with him. Apparently, now that he's married and his wife wants a child, he remembered that he has one he can use as a prop in his life …"

Fury laced every word Victoria spoke, and I felt it as sharply as if it were mine. My hands curled into fists as anger rose inside me, hot and relentless .

"He did *what?*" I repeated slowly, unable to believe what I was hearing.

"Yeah," Victoria said. "He came to her place twice. Threatened her. Amelia is terrified. She's staying with her parents for a while, trying to figure out what she's going to do."

The tension inside me coiled tighter, like a spring ready to snap. "Why didn't she tell me? I want to be there for her. I want to help her through this."

Victoria's sigh came again, heavy and almost tired. "Because she doesn't want to be an inconvenience. She knows you have important games coming up, and she doesn't want you distracted. And she also doesn't want you to miss out on an important transfer because of her. She's trying to protect you from worrying."

I ran my hands through my hair, frustration and helplessness mixing into a bitter taste in my mouth. "Then why didn't she consider moving in with me? I'd be more than happy to have both her and Sophie. I'd make sure they're safe and that they're okay. I'd do anything for them."

Even as I said it aloud, I felt it in my bones. I had known this for months, deep down in my heart. Amelia was it for me. There was no one else. No one else in this world would ever take her place. As simple and as terrifying as that thought was, it was the truth I couldn't ignore.

"Brad really scared her," Victoria said, her voice low but firm. "The threats he made weren't a joke. I'm guessing she was afraid he might do something to you, too. As I said, this has nothing to do with you. Amelia has already gone through such a traumatic experience with him, and now she's forced to face it all over again. I'm sure that once it's all sorted out, she'll reach out and try to explain, maybe even try to fix things. Right now, she's acting out of panic."

Her words hung in the air, but I barely processed them. My mind was racing, tangled with anger, frustration, and an overwhelming need to act.

First, I wanted to get my hands on that bastard who had terrified her.

Second, I didn't want Amelia to wait until everything settled before reaching out. I wanted her to know I was there for her now, when she needed me the most.

And third, despite the chaos in my career, despite everything, I wanted to see her. As soon as possible.

"Diego?" Victoria's voice pulled me back.

"Yeah," I said, my words tight and hurried. "I hear you. I have to go now, but can you please keep me updated on what's happening with her?"

"I—"

"Thank you." I hung up before the conversation could go any further. I didn't have time for explanations or reassurances. My mind was already made up. I knew how important the next game was. My coach, manager, and teammates were all counting on me. And yet, deep in my chest, I knew what mattered more. I had a choice: I could play for my club right now, or I could go to the woman who had stolen my heart.

With that clarity, I headed into my bedroom. I pulled out one of my suitcases and began packing only the essentials: clothes, toiletries, and a few personal items. Everything else

I could buy in Houston. I was planning to stay there for as long as it took until she was safe and secure. Nothing else mattered.

I took one last look at my phone and tossed it onto the bed as a strange sense of calm settled over me. I would text my coach later. Surely he would understand that their safety came before anything else. Right now, there was only one thing I needed to do.

I had to follow my heart.

Thirty
Amelia

I knew better than to ever take Brad lightly. The more I thought about everything that had happened between us, the more uneasy I became. Brad had always been the kind of man who chased after what he wanted, and he never stopped until he got it. It didn't matter if it was business, pleasure, or something in between.

And this time, Sophie was the one thing I couldn't let him have.

"Mommy? What's wrong?" a small voice piped up behind me, snapping me out of my thoughts. I turned and forced a smile, trying to hide the storm that was building inside me. My little girl didn't deserve to carry the weight of adult worries.

"Nothing, pumpkin …" I lied gently. The words tasted bitter, but what else could I say? "Mommy just has a few things on her mind, that's all. Nothing for you to worry that pretty little head about, okay?" I added, brushing a strand of hair from her face and keeping that smile plastered on, even though my heart felt heavy.

I looked Brad up online again after our encounter. I'd done it a few times over the years, to see where life had taken him. For the longest time, there wasn't much to find, but that changed about a year ago, when he married the daughter of an energy tycoon. She was a woman from a family so wealthy that I couldn't even begin to picture their world.

He had power now and connections that could open doors I wanted to stay tightly shut. I knew Brad well enough to understand that he wouldn't hesitate to use them if he thought it would help him get what he wanted. The idea of him trying to take Sophie from me made my head throb and my stomach twist.

"Mommy …" Sophie's soft voice pulled me back again.

I crouched down so I was eye level with her. "Hey, sweetheart," I said quietly, reaching out to tuck her hand into mine. "How about we get out of here for a bit? Maybe go for some ice cream?"

Her eyes lit up instantly, all traces of worry forgotten. Within seconds, she ran off to grab her little backpack, her laughter echoing down the hallway.

I watched her go, as my chest tightened even more. Coming to my parents' house after running into Brad again had felt like the safest option. It didn't feel right to keep Sophie locked up here, even if the familiar walls of my childhood surrounded us.

I grabbed my purse and car keys, sweeping my gaze over the counter for my phone when the doorbell suddenly rang. I froze mid-step, my breath catching in my throat. For a moment, everything around me went still. I had been living on edge for days; every unexpected sound made my heart race. The thought that Brad might show up here, at my parents' doorstep, demanding to see Sophie, haunted me constantly.

Heavy footsteps moved across the hardwood floor as my mother went to answer the door. We had talked about this exact moment and had planned for it. If Brad ever came here, she would tell him I wasn't home and threaten to call the police. I prayed that would be enough to send him away if he was foolish enough to show up unannounced.

I stood completely still, straining to hear what was happening in the living room. Muffled voices drifted in, followed by two sets of footsteps. My pulse quickened. Then the doorway filled with a familiar figure. *Diego.*

For a second, I couldn't move. My chest tightened, and my lips parted, but no words came out. Of all people, he was the last one I expected to see standing there. Before I could even speak, Sophie burst out of the guest room, her face lighting up like the sun.

"Diego!" she squealed, running straight toward him.

He crouched down and scooped her up, spinning her effortlessly in his arms. Sophie's laughter filled the air, and I felt something deep inside me loosen that I hadn't even realized had been clenched so tight. Diego's expression, though, told a different story. His smile was warm for Sophie's sake, but his eyes were full of worry.

I didn't understand why he was here. After the way I ended things between us, he had every reason to stay away. But that didn't make it hurt any less.

"Hey, Soph," Diego said softly, smiling at her. "I've missed you."

"I missed you too!" she giggled, wrapping her little arms around his neck. "Mommy said you wouldn't be visiting anytime soon. So how come you came?"

Diego lifted his gaze to mine. "Mommy was wrong. I'm right here, and I'm not going anywhere."

Almost as if she could sense the tension hanging in the air, my mom stepped in, her voice calm and warm. "Soph, sweetheart, why don't you come with me? Let's go get some cookies so your mom can talk to Diego for a minute."

That was all it took to grab Sophie's attention. Diego gently set her down, and in an instant, she was off, her little feet pattering down the hallway toward the kitchen. My mom gave me a quick, knowing look before following her, leaving me standing there in the wreckage of my emotions.

The moment they were gone, it all hit me like a wave. My throat tightened, and the familiar burn behind my eyes came fast. I blinked hard, trying to fight it back, but it was no use. The tears gathered anyway, shimmering at the edge before spilling over.

"What are you doing here?" I managed, my voice trembling despite my best effort to steady it. "The season—"

"The season doesn't matter," Diego cut in firmly. "Not for now, at least. I let my coach know I'd be missing a few games while I help you figure this out. He understood. Victoria told me what happened. Why you ended things." He took a slow breath, his gaze never leaving mine. "I just wish you'd come to me instead of shutting me out. But I get it. You were scared. You did what you thought was best." He stepped a little closer, his voice lowering. "You've been handling everything on your own for so long that it's the only way you know how to survive. But it doesn't have to be like that anymore. You don't have to face this alone. If you'd just let me in, I'll be there for you. I'll help you through this. I'll help you through anything."

Some of his words blurred together as I fought to keep my composure, but the tears won anyway. They streamed down my face freely. Guilt hit me so hard it stole the air from my lungs. The ache in my chest was sharp, deep, and entirely my own doing. I had broken this. I had pushed him away.

"I'm sorry," I whispered, my voice cracking. "There's just a lot happening. I didn't know how to deal with any of it." I wiped my face with the back of my hand, trying to steady myself. "Brad's been threatening to take Sophie from me. And it scared the hell out of me. She's my little girl, Diego. She's everything I have. I couldn't let myself get distracted, not when he's out there trying to take her away."

"I don't have to be a distraction," he said finally, his voice low and steady. "I can be an ally, too. Someone to stand by your side when things get hard, but only if you let me."

A sob threatened to rise from my chest, and I fought it back with everything I had. It had been easier when he wasn't standing this close. But right now, with his eyes on me and his words reaching places I'd buried deep, all those walls began to crumble.

He could see it happening. I knew he could.

Before I could stop myself, he stepped forward and wrapped his arms around me. The moment his arms closed around my body, something inside me broke. The dam I'd built up over days gave way, and I let go.

I buried my face in his chest, sobbing into the warmth of him. Every bit of fear, frustration, and guilt came pouring out, muffled against his shirt. He didn't try to hush me or pull away. He just held me tighter, one hand cradling the back of my head, the other resting gently against my back.

I had never had this before. I had never had someone who didn't try to fix everything—someone who just *stayed* and made the world feel a little less impossible by simply being there.

I didn't know how long he held me—minutes, maybe more. Time blurred until the sobs faded into quiet sniffles and my breathing steadied. Only then did Diego tilt my chin up, his fingers gentle against my skin, his eyes searching mine.

"I don't accept our breakup," he said. "You can end things if your feelings change, or if you really don't want to be with me anymore. But I'm not letting Brad stand in the way of what we have. Let me help you. Let me be here with you."

I opened my mouth, the same protest slipping out automatically. "But your season—"

He smiled faintly, shaking his head. "As I said, it doesn't matter. Or, well, it does—but not more than you. Not more than Sophie. The sooner you understand that, the better."

He reached up, brushing a stray strand of hair behind my ear with a tenderness that made my heart ache. Then he leaned in, closing the distance between us. His lips met mine in a slow, gentle kiss.

I melted into him, kissing him back with everything I had—every bit of longing and fear and love I'd tried to bury. It felt like breathing again after being underwater too long. In that moment, for the first time in what felt like forever, I let myself believe maybe I didn't have to fight this battle alone.

Thirty-One
Diego

Sophie hopped down from the car, her hand slipping into mine as she looked up with a tiny pout. "I thought we were going to stay with Nana and Papa longer."

Across the hood, Amelia locked the doors and raised an eyebrow at me. I knew she would have stayed there forever if I let her. They made her feel safe.

But I'd already made my decision hours earlier when I texted my coach: I would be taking a short leave for the next few games. Just enough time to be here—really be here—for Amelia and Sophie.

He didn't fight me on it. Didn't question or pressure me. He just said, *"Take the time you need. Family comes first."*

The support hit harder than I expected, loosening something tight in my chest. I had spent years believing my whole world revolved around soccer, but in that moment, knowing my coach had my back… I felt nothing but gratitude.

"Well," I said, swinging Amelia's bag over my shoulder, "we figured we could go back to your apartment. I'll be staying with you girls for a little while. How does that sound?"

Sophie's entire face lit up. "For real? Oh goodness! You still have a lot to teach me, you know—I showed my friends the tricks and they LOVED them."

Her excitement tugged a laugh out of me. "Lucky for you, I've got plenty more."

"Can you show me now?" she asked instantly.

Before I could answer, Amelia was already unlocking the apartment door. "Absolutely not, missy."

Sophie puffed her cheeks out dramatically, arms crossed. I crouched down, trying not to smile.

"Maybe tomorrow," I offered. "Deal?"

"Maybe…" she drawled, then broke into a smile.

She disappeared to wash her hands, her footsteps fading down the hall. As soon as she was out of sight, I stepped behind Amelia and wrapped my arms around her waist, pulling her gently back against me. I kissed the side of her neck.

"My God, I missed you," I murmured. "These past few days have been hell."

Her body softened instantly. I turned her to face me, brushing my thumb along her cheek.

"I missed you too," she whispered, rising on her toes to kiss me. "So much."

I leaned my forehead to hers. "Don't try to handle everything alone anymore, okay? But if you ever do have to run…" I tilted her chin. "Run into me."

Her small, quiet smile, meant only for me, settled something deep inside my chest.

The next morning, Amelia went back to work after I insisted, she didn't need to take more time off. I stayed home with Sophie, dropped her off at school, straightened up the apartment a little, and thought about dinner… simple things that somehow meant more than anything I'd done in years.

For the first time in my life, my day revolved around something other than soccer and training. The quiet apartment felt like a preview of a life I didn't know I wanted until it was right here in front of me. A life that felt calm. Real. Ours.

My agent texted, asking if I had made a final decision.

Private reasons, I replied.

I needed just a little more time. He understood, and I was grateful for people who actually cared.

On the way to pick up Sophie, I stopped for a bouquet of pink lilies, Amelia's favorite. After the last few days, she had, she deserved every soft thing in the world.

Houston wasn't Miami. The streets were slower, unfamiliar. But driving through them, headed toward a little girl who trusted me and a woman who had cracked me open in ways I never saw coming, I felt something I hadn't felt in a very long time.

Peace.

When I reached the school, I stepped out, leaning against the hood as the crowd of parents shifted around the gate. Sophie appeared, backpack bouncing, and my smile started before I could stop it.

Then I saw him.

Brad.

Every muscle in me went tight in an instant. Sophie spotted me and started toward me, but Brad's arm moved across her shoulder, stopping her.

"Come here, Sophie," he said.

My vision narrowed. I stepped forward slowly—not rushing, not shouting, letting every ounce of controlled fury pour into the space between us.

"Let her go," I said.

He rolled his eyes. "Relax, man—"

I stepped closer, close enough that he could see I wasn't playing games.

"Let. Her. Go."

Something in my tone reached him. He let her go.

Sophie ran to me, and I crouched down, keeping my eyes locked on Brad. "Hop in the car, sweetheart. We'll get ice cream, okay?"

She beamed and hurried off, leaving the two of us standing alone in a swirl of parents and kids.

I rose to my full height.

"You don't get to do this," I said. "You walked out on her. You walked out on *both* of them."

He scoffed. "You don't know anything—"

"You're right," I cut in. "I don't know why a man abandons his child before she's even born. I don't know how someone disappears for years and thinks he can just stroll back when it's convenient."

I stepped closer.

"But I do know this: Amelia isn't someone you get to toy with anymore. Sophie isn't someone you get to confuse or use as leverage. They have me now. *This* is my family. And I will protect them. Do you understand?"

He smirked. "Okay, superstar. We'll see about that."

"Oh, you will," I said. "Soon."

I turned away from him, got into the car, and dialed the number I knew by heart.

The call connected.

"Mitchell," came Ron Mitchell's deep voice, one of the best lawyers in Miami.

"It's Diego," I said. "I need help. Serious help. I want this handled fast."

"Whatever you need," he replied without hesitation. "Say the word. You have my full support."

Relief and purpose settled in my chest. "Done deal."

I hung up and glanced back. Sophie was singing, swinging her legs, completely unaware of the storm that had just passed.

"Ready for ice cream?" I asked gently.

"Yes!" she squealed.

We grabbed her favorite cone and headed home.

When we pulled into the driveway, Amelia was already at the door, one hand braced against the frame, the late-afternoon light catching her hair. She looked tired, relieved, beautiful.

Sophie unbuckled herself before I even parked and launched herself toward her.

"Mommy!"

They embraced, Amelia closing her eyes as Sophie wrapped her arms around her neck. Watching them stirred something fierce and tender in my chest.

I walked up the steps. Amelia looked at me over Sophie's shoulder, her eyes soft and grateful. She reached her hand out to me. I took it.

She leaned in, kissed me once—slow, warm, like a quiet thank you.

Sophie rushed inside, already talking about sprinkles and caramel drizzle. Amelia stayed with me in the doorway, her hands sliding up my chest.

"You know what I was thinking about today?" she asked softly.

I brushed a thumb beneath her jaw. "What's that, amor?"

She smiled. "England."

My chest warmed instantly, deep and certain.

"Oh yeah?" I murmured. "England."

She nodded, eyes bright with something that looked like hope. "I don't think it would be such a bad idea after all."

And standing in the doorway of a home that wasn't mine but felt like mine anyway, with the woman I loved pressed against me and the little girl who trusted me laughing somewhere inside—I knew.

Whatever came next was only the beginning of the best part of our lives.

Epilogue
Amelia

Six Months Later

"We won!"

Sophie shrieked as she burst through the front door, her red-and-white jersey bouncing with every excited step. She wore it like it was made of gold. If she loved anything in the world, it was cheering for Diego, and the pride on her face made it clear the night had gone perfectly.

"Woooooo!" she yelled, racing laps around the coffee table, hopping up and down while clapping wildly. I glanced over at Diego, and the grin that spread across my face was impossible to hide.

"I told you those donuts were a terrible idea at this hour," I teased, nudging him lightly. But if there was ever a night to spoil ourselves, it was tonight. Life had been throwing changes at us left and right, but for once, every single one seemed to land exactly where it needed to. It felt like the universe had finally stopped pushing against us.

"Alright, alright," Diego chuckled, reaching out to scoop Sophie closer and ruffle her hair. "It's nine p.m., kiddo. Time to start getting ready for bed."

Sophie froze mid-bounce, planted her feet, and crossed her arms.

"You still owe me and Mr. Buttons a story," she declared with complete seriousness. "You didn't read one yesterday." Her little face tried so hard to stay stern that it almost made me laugh.

"I know, I know. I had practice yesterday, remember?" Diego said, trying to defend himself.

Soph just lifted her tiny shoulders. "And? I get busy too, and I still spend time with you," she said, grinning wide enough to show the new tooth just beginning to peek through.

"You know what? You're right," he admitted. "That wasn't fair of me. How about this—go get ready for bed, and tonight we'll have a full audience."

Sophie raised an eyebrow, already hooked.

"I'll gather every single one of your stuffed animals," he promised, "and they'll all be there to listen."

That did it. She lit up instantly and dashed down the hall, then up the stairs.

I moved to follow Sophie, but Diego gave a small shake of his head. "I got this," he murmured as he leaned in and pressed a gentle kiss to my forehead. "Why don't you relax for a bit?"

I watched him climb the wooden staircase, slow and steady, the steps creaking just slightly beneath him. When he disappeared around the corner, I took another look around our new home. Even after six whole months, it still felt like some kind of dream we hadn't woken up from.

The warm beige walls were covered in endless photographs of moments we never wanted to forget, interspersed with Sophie's bright, messy paintings. The massive couch stretched across the living room, already broken in from cozy nights in. The kitchen glowed softly behind it, and our big wooden dining table sat waiting for the people we loved, even if they'd have to cross an ocean to get to us. My parents were already talking about flying in for the holidays, which warmed something deep inside me.

London.

Just thinking the word still sent a strange little shiver through me—part disbelief, part gratitude. Ever since Diego came back into our lives, it was like everything had finally started to settle into place. Brad had faded from our orbit again, swallowed by his own chaos. The news hinted at lawsuits, whispers of trouble, but nothing concrete. I suspected his wife stepped in long before it spiraled.

For once, the mess wasn't ours to clean up.

Little by little, Sophie and I had started breathing freely again. The apartment felt lighter, our mornings weren't weighed down by fear anymore, and nights didn't feel so long or quiet with Diego asleep beside me. He told me he'd stay as long as I needed—until I felt safe again. But even then, guilt tugged at me. I didn't want him sacrificing his dreams for us.

So, one night, I let myself really sit with it.

England wasn't impossible. It was a beginning.

A chance.

A doorway to a life that didn't rely on fear or survival.

When I shared the idea with Sophie, expecting nerves, she lit up like I had handed her a golden ticket. She was in.

And because of her, so was I.

Diego accepted his Premier League transfer, stepped into this new chapter with confidence, and the three of us packed up our lives and crossed the ocean together.

My phone buzzed in my purse. I smiled the moment I saw the caller ID.

I answered, and immediately Victoria and Anastasia filled my screen—faces bright, dramatic, chaotic in their perfect way.

"Hey, girl!" Victoria squealed. "What's going on across the pond today?"

I laughed. "The sweet taste of victory! We just got home from a game. Diego won, and Sophie's on a sugar high. He's handling bedtime."

"A king," Anastasia said, nodding. "And you? Have you been adjusting, okay?"

"I am," I admitted. "The only thing missing is my girls…"

Anastasia's expression softened. "And work? How's that been?"

Work had been one of the biggest pieces of the puzzle when we decided to move. Mr. Thompson had been sad to see me go, but he didn't hesitate to put in a good word for me with a sister company in London. Thanks to him, I had a position waiting for me—something I loved and was actually good at. Sometimes it felt unreal how smoothly everything had fallen into place, as if the universe had finally stopped fighting me and started clearing the path.

Victoria smirked. "Good. Because the Three Musketeers are taking England this spring. You better warn the locals."

Anastasia gasped dramatically. "And the pastries."

I laughed so hard my stomach hurt. Even from across an ocean, our connection never felt stronger. Their voices wrapped around me like a familiar blanket, easing the last bit of homesickness I didn't even realize I was still carrying

When we finally said goodbye, the screen went dark, leaving the room warm and quiet.

Moments later, Diego came down the stairs. "We ended up doing three bedtime stories," he sighed, collapsing beside me. I curled into him immediately as he wrapped an arm around me, pulling me close.

"She drove a hard bargain today, didn't she?" I murmured.

"You have no idea," he said, kissing my forehead. His fingers traced slow, lazy shapes along my arm, easing every last knot out of my chest.

"What are you thinking about?" he whispered.

"Nothing much," I breathed. "Just that this is our life right now, it feels unbelievable."

He hummed. "More or less."

I tilted my head in question, and he smiled—soft, shy, almost nervous in a way I rarely saw.

"I do intend on making a few changes," he said quietly. "Like giving you both my last name—if you'll have it."

Before I could process the warmth flooding my chest, he reached into the pocket of his sweats and pulled out a small velvet box.

My breath vanished.

He opened it, the ring catching the warm glow of the lamp.

"When I met you in Vegas," he began softly, "I had no idea my life would end up here—playing in the Premier League, living in England, and falling asleep every night with you and Sophie under the same roof. Nothing ever felt real before you. You two… you're the meaning I didn't know I was missing."

Emotion surged up my throat, sharp and overwhelming.

He held the ring gently between us, his voice low and steady.

"I've been a lot of places, Amelia… but the only place that's ever felt right is next to you and Sophie."

His fingers threaded through mine.

"Will you marry me?"

A breathless laugh escaped me—half sob, half pure joy.

"Yes," I whispered. "Yes."

He slipped the ring onto my finger, pulling me into his arms as I laughed and cried into his neck. He held me like he'd been waiting his whole life to do it.

"You're my home," I whispered.

"And you're mine," he murmured, kissing me slow and sure.

The view of London glowed softly beyond our glass windows, a quiet reminder of how far we'd come. In his arms, with the ring glistening in the warm light of our home, everything finally felt exactly as it should. For the first time in my life, I wasn't bracing for something to go wrong.

I wasn't waiting for the moment someone left.

I was staying.

Choosing.

Letting myself be loved, fully and fearlessly.

And as Diego held me close, the future didn't just look possible—it finally felt like something I could reach for.

With him.

With Sophie.

With the life we were building — finally, beautifully, ours.

Acknowledgments

To my daughter: thank you for being the brightest reason. You have been the inspiration behind my writing journey from the very beginning, my spark for children's books and beyond. Everything I write is touched by you. You are, and will always be, my greatest motivation.

To my sister, who listens to every idea and never hesitates to give her input, thank you for being the best big sister a girl could have. Sofia and I are so grateful to have such a fun, loving aunt in our lives.

To my friends, who I adore, thank you for listening, encouraging, and reminding me to keep going. You carried me more than you know. I cherish each of you.

To my parents, my biggest cheerleaders, thank you for rooting for me every step of the way. I love you, and I hope I have made you proud.

And to every reader who picked up this book, and to those who supported my earlier children's books, thank you. Thank you for taking a chance on my debut, for letting these characters find a place in your heart and on your bookshelf. Thank you for being part of the beginning of this journey. I hope this story meets you gently, exactly where you need it.

About the Author

Samantha Miller was born and raised in Houston, Texas. She is the author of three children's books, each inspired by her experience as a devoted mother and her desire to bring comfort, confidence, and connection to young readers. Her early work reflects the realities of balancing work and motherhood, and the deep bond between parent and child.

Now stepping into new creative territory, Samantha makes her romance debut, bringing the same heart, emotion, and honesty to her adult fiction.

Samantha works as a Social Media Marketing Director, a role that allows her creativity and love of storytelling to extend beyond the page. When she's not writing, she enjoys spending time with family and friends, exploring music, travel, fitness, and dreaming up the next story she can't wait to share.

You can find her on social media at @smpublishingco